Wedding Day Massacre

Aron Beauregard

ISBN: 9798719650760

Cover & Interior Art by Anton Rosovsky

About the Author Art by Katherine Burns

Cover wrap design by Don Noble

Edited by Laura Wilkinson

Special Thanks to Mort Stone for Additional
Revisions

Printed in the USA

Maggot Press
Coventry, Rhode Island

WARNING:
This book contains scenes and subject matter
that are disgusting and disturbing, easily
offended people are not the intended audience

JOIN MY MAGGOT MAILING LIST NOW
FOR EXCLUSIVE OFFERS AND UPDATES
BY EMAILING
AronBeauregardHorror@gmail.com

WWW.EVILEXAMINED.COM

DEADICATION

To anyone who's engaged or already married. May your love stay strong and your lives remain free of horror and, most importantly, massacre…

"We're born alone, we live alone, we die alone. Only through our love and friendship can we create the illusion for the moment that we're not alone."

- Orson Welles

LOCATION, LOCATION, LOCATION

Sebastian and Taylor filed into the classy lobby of the Biltmore, intimately taking in the venue that would most certainly change their lives forever. Usually, the bride's parents would pay for the wedding, but Sebastian had insisted that they allow him to cover all expenses. He didn't want to take credit for it publicly but he'd gone out of his way to explain it on numerous occasions. He looked at their wedding as the ideal opportunity to show Taylor and her family how much he cared about them. He'd been saving for the day his entire life — it was in his head long before he found Taylor. Whomever fate saw fit to be Sebastian's soul mate would never need to worry about a thing.

Dorian, their wedding planner, poked the up button and waved them over just as the elevator arrived. "Right this way!" he said with a smile and enthusiasm that would've jumped out from the crowd had there been one. But the Biltmore was barren. No guests busily stirring about and rushing in and out. It was empty, all but for a pair of maids preparing a cleaning solution near the restroom.

Sebastian moseyed over with his arm tangled relaxingly with his soon-to-be trophy wife's. Sure, he'd just turned thirty-two but he was years ahead in maturity. A lifetime of excessively responsible, frugal, and more often than not, downright boring approaches had made the blueprint possible.

Carving out an administrative role for himself at an upstart internet advertising company had left his bank account with premier client branding. Pairing that personal stability with a sound knowledge of investments spawned the more than promising young man that was nearing the million-dollar mark staring back at him in the mirror every morning.

Taylor knew it wouldn't take him long to add another digit. But even more heart-pounding than Sebastian's already booming success was knowing that once they were married, part of that fortune would become hers too. There were now only a handful of formalities left separating her from a stress-less golden future.

She looked down at her phone as they entered the levitating cell: 117 new text messages, 302 new emails, and 36 missed calls. The novel-worth of communication was all from that day. The always social butterfly couldn't sleep a wink without clearing out the queue first. Taylor was a chameleon, it was all a progression for her — find the meal ticket, "fall in love," enjoy the wedding and festivities that lead up to it, then, when the time is right, cash out.

As they ascended, stimulating imagery populated her skull; high fashion, stardom, indulgence. And the best part was that she would be at the center of it all.

Taylor knew she deserved so much more than the mediocracy that had been allotted to her, and finally, it was only a cunt hair away. The outline of her carefully premeditated and monetarily fruitful future dispelled her depression and raised her psyche to scream-worthy heights like a potent drug splashing into her bloodstream.

She leaned up against the wall as she watched the floor indicator continue upwards. A well-acted and believable abuse scandal followed up by a few court dates would see her quickly rid herself of the pale fat boy, but not his surging wealth. She saw herself somewhere like southern California or maybe Florida, preparing for luxury and finding the dreamboat stud she'd sculpted while fantasizing during her finger-flick sessions.

She looked at Sebastian's chubby cheeks and pinched the left one, pulling him in for a kiss. Dorian waved his hand toward his collar as if to say, 'it's getting hot in here!'

Taylor didn't feel bad for him, mostly because she couldn't. It was one of the perks of being a sociopath. All she saw was the light at the end of the tunnel. A daiquiri in between her shimmering and snowy manicured fingertips and her toned to excess body caramelizing from excessive doses of religious poolside sunbathing.

3

The socialites would flock to a flashy persona such as hers at the gym or nightclubs. She'd be in the settings she'd daydreamt about, eventually acting as the new leader of a crass clique of people with a similar shallowness. The people she fancied and identified with. And it would all be happening in less than a year.

She didn't want to rush the plan and make it feel the slightest bit unnatural or questionable. She wanted to do things right, everything had to be perfect and it would be. Everyone knew the story, it's one that was true more often than not.

The story goes that a relationship is perfect, the man is everything any bloodsucking babe would kill for. Then they get married, and suddenly, something sinister begins to blossom. Suddenly, the charming man contorts into something entirely different. He's controlling. He's manipulative. He's demanding. He's aggressive. He's filled with pure rage. But most importantly, he's violent.

She already had a few ideas that might be a little painful, but each cut and bruise she manufactured upon her body would be accompanied by the sound of a cash register ringing. She would accumulate dozens of hushed incidents before letting the cat out of the bag. It didn't matter that Sebastian didn't have a history of violence. The talking heads always believed a woman.

An alert popped up on Taylor's cell, causing a vibration against her ass cheek. She fished the device back out again and examined it. There it was, a new 'Me Too' piece populating her screen.

The climate was a cog that fit perfectly into her plot-wheel. In an era rife with talk of female empowerment and a bloodlust for the slightest whiff of male misconduct, all she'd need to do was find the right shoulders to cry on and the pitchforks would come out stabbing.

She already had a large enough following to ensure the exposure would generate a scandal with some legs. If she posted the appropriate content to trigger the virtual mob and began to advocate for abused women "like herself," then Sebastian's prolific empire would come crumbling down at freefall speed.

Once she'd successfully vilified him, things would be close to a wrap. Taylor would be patiently left waiting to sift through the rubble and pick up the scraps. Those scraps would be beefy enough to vault her into a new stratosphere. She would quickly find herself in an existence of constant leisure and holiday.

She generated an internal sigh as she reassessed his attire—he was painfully plain. Sebastian was a square, more vanilla than the play calling of a pre-season football game. He was formal, intelligent, and sweet, but anyone who knew either of them could see from a mile away that something wasn't quite right about their arrangement.

Those who knew Taylor understood what the deal was, it wasn't like they needed to run the query: "So, why are you marrying a guy that is completely out of your league?" Before they even internally pondered the question, they'd found themselves reciting the answer: "Oh, the fucking money, of course."

The elevator finally came to a jerking halt and Sebastian and Taylor locked eyes once again before exiting. While they were both completely different, Taylor didn't hate being around him. He was robotic and dull but he always allowed her space. He never whined or complained or acted emotionally clingy in the slightest. Maybe that was what she liked most about him… she didn't really have to be around him at all.

Sebastian didn't get butthurt about the distance kept in the slightest. She was a ghost anywhere from four to five nights a week. Bar-hopping, flirting, getting wild with her girls, and fucking raw with a reckless abandon were just a few of the things that she was always free to do.

The level of wild unadulterated liberation was remarkable. The type that a drop-dead hottie like herself wasn't accustomed to. Nearly every other guy she'd ever been with tried to pin her under their thumb, knowing that the second they left her side, some suave cocksucker at the bar doused in cheap cologne would be buying her a martini and hoping for sex on the beach.

There had even been a handful of evenings that she didn't return home at all, yet somehow, there was no reaction on Sebastian's behalf. It bothered him so little that it was after one of these evening benders of Taylor's that he planted one knee on the Maison hand-knotted rug and popped the question.

She'd become so outwardly comfortable with her debauchery that she hadn't even had a chance to wash the dried cum shots from her highlights before she saw him. The moment happened quicker than she'd expected, but at the rate they were going, she could count on being finished with the whole charade even faster than initially anticipated.

The potential ballroom was on the 13th floor, which the Biltmore considered the 14th presumably due to old superstition. Dorian moved forward, leading the cheerful couple down the hallway and up to the already open doors.

They'd both rushed into the planning, eager for their own reasons. Sebastian offered to let her choose everything, and price wasn't an issue. After all, it was her special day. He'd even sought out Dorian to be at her disposal.

Dorian was one of the highest-rated wedding planners in the entire country as evidenced by the smorgasbord of five-star reviews that Sebastian had screenshotted and presented to her from years past. He would see to it that their ceremony was as modern and majestic as it could possibly be.

Dorian knew that the lone request Sebastian had asked Taylor to consider was the reception venue. The old hotel was a spot that he'd grown fond of in a love at first sight kind of way. A place that held deep nostalgia for him. A place he'd stayed at with his family as a child.

Understanding the importance of coming to an agreement, Dorian speedily arranged the viewing. Now that they were both in front of it together, he would be eager to learn what Taylor's take was. Once he knew how she felt, he could start getting on with the rest of the major preparations. Based on everything else Taylor had been blabbing about, he knew that almost any detail of the wedding was not going to be an easy sell.

"This place is just… it's breathtaking. Just like I remembered it," Sebastian gushed unsurprisingly.

Dorian perked up, excited by his reconfirmation.

He knew it brought them one step closer to locking down the location. He knew a place as ostentatious as the Biltmore Hotel should generate immediate infatuation, but he also knew Sebastian hadn't seen it in years. He was relieved to validate that his opinion hadn't wavered.

"This venue is fabulous, absolutely to die for. You can literally do anything you want in a space like this. This is exactly where I'd be getting married if it was up to me," he said, smiling at Sebastian.

Dorian turned back to Taylor, "But the important question is, what does the soon-to-be missus think?" The queerness in his voice was flamboyant. The look of wonder cast upon him asked if he might be in for his easiest sell in history that morning.

"If there is any doubt, I would also add that the hotel hasn't even officially relaunched yet. There will be no guests here to bother you, no unnecessary distractions. Getting a venue like this entirely to yourself is, well, it's unheard of. Just you, your guests, and a few of the hotel staff. In all my years of planning, I've never seen the stars align like this for a client." He was laying it on thick, but at the same time, he wasn't lying. The setup was legendary, truly once in a lifetime.

Tears started to well up in Taylor's eyes and a grin of excitement manifested below. Her wedding would be so much better than anyone else's. The beauty of the venue would stop just short of matching her own. People would comment on the event endlessly and she would gain an incredible amount of clout as an influencer with a nuptial that bordered on royalty. The event would be talked about FOREVER.

No one in her cynical circle would ever have the financial aptitude, resources, or flat-out luck to outdo it. It would be a celebration for the ages. The salty warm water began pouring down her cheeks. All eyes would be on her.

"Well then, it looks like we have our answer," Dorian confirmed with a smile of his own stretching ear to ear.

THAT SPECIAL DAY

It's the day everyone dreams about, the day that everyone wants to be perfect. For both Sebastian and Taylor, so far it had been. What started as a gorgeous outdoor autumn ceremony by the water had moved into the sophisticated age-old ballroom on the 13th floor of the Biltmore.

"So, why did you pick this place, baby? You never really told me," Taylor's inquiry didn't seem out of legitimate interest, more just a filler question to occupy the dead air before they entered.

"I mostly just enjoy the privacy... you know, being detached from it all. From the real world. Even if it's only temporary. Whenever my family stayed up this way to go skiing, we always slept here.

Which wasn't often really, but I guess it's like they say, absence makes the heart grow fonder."

"How are you gonna grow fonder of me when I'm always around you?" Her lies were convincing. She winked in a slutty way at him, it seemed like that was the only way she knew.

"It wouldn't even be possible to grow fonder of you, I love you too much already." His smile was glowing, Sebastian seemed even more at peace than he normally did.

Taylor wrapped her hands around his belly as they pulled in tightly for the fakest of hugs.

"The history is quite fascinating too," Sebastian said as he curved his arms around her, listening to the chatter of the crowd that could be heard through the ballroom doors.

"History?"

"Yeah, this place was constructed in 1922, but just a few decades ago, it abruptly fell into abandonment. But eventually, due to the building's rich history, there was a push to revive it. Places such as this, not too far from the mountains, have a lucrative appeal. After several restoration efforts, they're finally able to unlock the doors again."

"Why did it even close at all? Seems kind of dumb knowing how gorgeous it is firsthand. I mean, this place is a *total* cash cow."

"Some kind of accident happened. They got some bad press. But I think overall poor management seemed like the prime culprit. This place is too special to let anything keep it from being available to the public."

"Tell me about it, babe, can you believe we have it all to ourselves?"

"Nope, it still feels like a dream to me. I can't believe we're the first guests to set foot inside again, either. It's unreal. I can feel this… this buzz inside. The constructional face-lift has really modernized it but without painting over the vintage charm you see in the old photos," he said, breaking away from her and pointing to some of the black and white framed pictures on the wall beside them.

Taylor's mouth opened to respond but the music hit before she could and the doors in front of them flew open. They stepped out into the applauding mass of family and friends. The sight of the grand room, prepped exactly as they requested, would have reduced any hidden-agenda-less woman to tears.

Taylor reprocessed the surroundings again just as she had when they initially scoped it out. The magnificence of the location hadn't been watered down by a second viewing. If anything, it looked even more awe-inspiring. The guests buzzed back and forth through the two main doors that served as both entries and exits in between the main bar area.

The glee embroidered upon the faces of their attendees was overly evident as they began to find seating and retrieved their placeholders. She could tell they were all so glad to be there. Each individual couldn't have felt more honored to be a part of their breathtaking ceremony and to have a seat at such a spectacle of extravagance. Little did they know, for the greater majority, it would be the last party they'd ever attend.

CHICKEN OR FISH?

Uncle Ivan sat down at the table with the rest of the family. Everyone had turned out to witness the only next male son or nephew of the Zaluski clan get hitched. Sebastian had only invited the single table of family members in addition to a few scattered friends. The majority of the three hundred or so attendees were from the vast plethora of too-cool-for-school trendsetters that Taylor influenced with and those in her family tree (which was so extensive, it was more like a forest).

The second-generation Slavic-American family was a modest and hardworking bunch. While Sebastian's parents, aunts, and uncles had all been raised in the United States, they arrived late enough to keep a foreign tinge to their accents which caused them to charmingly omit a necessary word from

13

their speech here or there.

Their banter always sounded entertaining and Sebastian enjoyed their arguments. While they all whole-heartedly loved America, they still carried over many of the traditions that had been ingrained from the old country.

They were alike in many ways, but none of them had ever been able to replicate the success that so effortlessly overflowed from Sebastian. He was the golden boy. A much more cerebral creature than the rest of his bloodline who exuded a more rugged hands-on mentality.

Sebastian was excited that all members of his limited family would be present for the wedding. It was something that he clearly conveyed was quite important to him. His father, Zander, sat sandwiched between his mother, Hana, and uncle, Ivan, who had just taken his seat with what would regretfully but indisputably be the first of many vodka tonics.

Ivan's fourth wife, Olga, looked on in silence but with disapproval while their teenage daughter, Nina, obliviously rounded out the table, fiddling on her phone. They had all seen this show before and they knew how it ended—Ivan gets sloshed, says ignorant things, and makes a total ass of himself.

"Getting started early, Ivan? Very nice. Hope you reserve Uber already." Zander eyed Ivan's tall drink, going in on his embattled brother's bout with alcoholism from the jump.

"I have designated driver," he rebutted, looking over toward his wife, Olga.

"Drink too many and that may not be truth." Olga's English was fractured but it cut right to the point. She didn't appear to be in the mood for any of his typical horseshit.

"You know, I never thought we'd see this day," Ivan said, changing the subject to ignore his wife.

"Why is that?" Zander asked.

"Because I never see Sebastian with girl, just work, work, work. I always thought your boy like other boys. I always thought he is faggot."

"You drunk pig! Keep your mouth shut! Or it won't be just the drink that knock you out tonight!"

"Oh, brother, I know you wish you could. But you know as well as I, you cannot have wedding without best man." Ivan grinned as he reached deep into his inside pocket and retrieved a small box.

"You must be very jealous. Your son make me part of wedding, while you must only sit and watch." A vile laughter erupted. His hoarse cackle sounded almost as disgusting as the pleasure he derived from his brother's gloom. The hurt and rage blazed around Zander.

"Enough! You both stop! And, Ivan, you have respect for my son's wedding or I promise the night will not be well to you," Hana interjected.

"I'm not sure why Sebastian even wanted to come back to this place after the last time we were here…" Ivan continued.

"What happened last time?" Nina asked, finally finding interest in something besides her phone.

The waiter approached before anyone at their table could answer. A cheesy smile stuck to his face as he spoke, "Hello there, folks, so what's it going to be tonight, chicken or fish?"

OPEN BAR

The event was worth crashing just for the reward of the booze alone. Cindy was considering blowing off the evening altogether until Paula convinced her that she would never be forgiven.

"Taylor would've found a way to get you back. Skipping out when she made you a part of the wedding is a cardinal sin. One that you would have lived to regret forever," explained Paula.

"Nobody needs me. Stupid formalities. You're a fucking bridesmaid too. She would've had one still," Cindy replied, glancing behind the bar again.

She argued but knew Paula was right, which was why she ultimately showed up. Cindy didn't want to rock the boat and, in turn, have a vindictive little bitch like Taylor scanning endlessly for the next window of revenge.

Taylor was incredibly talented at finding ways to ruin special things if motivated to. Even though it was a hangover, not some malicious intent that was squashing her desire to attend the reception, none of that mattered. There were no excuses with a girl like Taylor, this is how "friends" in their circle thought — in a cycle of fear.

Thankfully, she was glad she'd come. Not just for the alleviation of any ill will, but also the open bar and overall epic presentation of the event. After two drinks, the harsh troubles of the prior night's alcohol poisoning had vanished and she was on her way to two nights in a row! She threw back the entire cosmo in a single gulp and batted her eyes at the bartender, as if showing off her swallowing technique.

"I'd fuck the shit outta him," Cindy confided in Paula without filter.

"What does that phrase even mean? I never really understood it or took a moment to think about it. Is it implying that you'd fuck long enough to actually shit yourself?"

"It's a great question, I think it's about making the other person shit *themselves* though. Fucking the shit out of yourself would have to be a solo effort but, to your point, I've had some marathons in my heyday and never had a guy shit for me."

"Me neither…"

"Should it feel a little disheartening? Because that's kinda what I'm getting now… Are we just another couple of inadequates?" Cindy's joke was just that. They both shared a roaring laugh for a tick, yet somehow, a smarting melancholic feeling of insufficiency legitimately began creeping into the atmosphere.

"So, let's place our bets, what's the expiration date on this thing? It already smells a little funky to me and it hasn't even started yet," Cindy asked, feeling it was best to swap the subject.

"Well, I think seeing that throughout this entire 'relationship' Taylor has nailed more wood than a carpenter, I'd give it six months. Seven tops. Is that fair?" Paula asked.

"Absolutely. Great minds think alike," Cindy said, knocking the edge of her glass a little harder than she needed to into Paula's.

Cindy took a big gulp of the drink and made a sound of elation before continuing. "That should be just enough time for her to get some money. I mean, look at this fuckin' guy, he's not her type. It doesn't make any sense. He's so nice and plain, she'll fucking ruin him."

"She already screwed it up with Don, he was no idiot. He knew exactly what she was up to. When that talk of a prenup started, she bailed with the quickness. I guarantee she gets her money this go around though," Paula surmised.

"See, here's the weirdest thing though. I think Sebastian is even smarter than Don was… I mean, he knows she's never around. He knows she's up to no good. If you're aware of that, why would you attach yourself to someone who's such an obvious pitfall?"

"I don't know, maybe he's just not the jealous type? Love can make people do some crazy shit, but more than likely it's because Taylor gives stupendous deepthroat and has a really nice ass."

"And a perfect tan…" Cindy continued, letting more than a smidge of jealousy surge.

"How does that bitch get her teeth so white? That smile…" Paula's disgust was an obvious self-reflection.

"She really does, I mean, look at her," they both paused for a moment, admiring the rear of her tight dress that made her figure pop. Then they moved onto the other checkmarks of sexiness that they'd just mentioned. Taylor was simply stunning, and the resentment amongst her girls was real.

As she clawed at Sebastian's tux seductively and they kissed, Cindy couldn't help but wonder aloud, "Why are we friends with such horrible people?"

"Because being around awful people makes us feel better about ourselves, you know this. Plus, it's a lot more entertaining. Being good just isn't any kind of fun…"

The bartender set a couple of fresh drinks in front of them and flashed his ridiculously perfect dimples for a quick second. "Drink up, I'm sure you already know, it's all on the house. If you get thirsty again, I'm your guy, I've got anything that the two of you beautiful girls want."

Paula and Cindy each set their empty glasses down and took hold of their new ones. Paula looked back to the attractive drink pourer, "I guarantee we'll be back, handsome. Maybe it'll be for more than just drinks next time…" Paula took Cindy by the hand and led her away.

"Where are we going? We're right where we need to be," Cindy wined but still slowly complied with the direction.

"Let's just go to the table for a few minutes, it looks like they're finally bringing out the food."

"But I legit think he could be the guy…"

"Who?"

"The one that finally shits for me," Cindy said, no longer joking.

Paula scrunched up her face as they closed in on their seats, "How romantic."

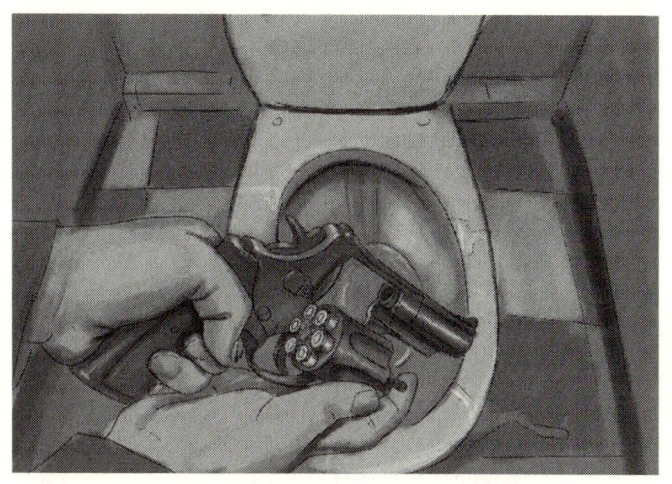

DADDY'S LITTLE GIRL

"I can't believe our little girl is all grown up now," Anthony Mazzarelli confided to his significant other, Lisa, as she shoveled another load of baked cod into her mouth. He stared across the room glossy-eyed as Taylor and Sebastian laughed playfully while finishing up their meals. He'd never seen her look so beautiful, which to him was saying a lot.

"He's a lucky man, a damn lucky man. Better treat her right or else he'll regret it."

"Of course he's going to treat her right, Anthony, he paid for all this, not us. He's been nothing but a complete gentleman since we've met him. Don't be so pessimistic," Lisa replied.

"Money isn't everything, Lisa. I mean, you're telling me that there isn't a small part of you that thinks this is a little too fast?"

"Honey, that's just Taylor, she's spontaneous. You know your daughter, when she sees something that she wants, she takes it. And no one, not even you can stop her. It's how she's always been."

Taylor's parents had aged with a grace that anyone would pray to. Their bronzed tone and fit physiques were what their daughter chose to emulate. They were also young at heart — they had to be to chase around and supervise a completely dependent nineteen-year-old.

They both loved children but weren't expecting what they'd ultimately received. In a move that was probably a premature knee-jerk reaction to Taylor starting to grow up, they decided to try and have a second child. Evading the void that their daughter's absence would eventually leave was something they tried to fix, maybe a little too early…

Christopher gulped down a swig of cola and puffed out his cheeks. He gargled for a moment before mumbling, "No one can stop her."

Unfortunately, their son was not what they were expecting. Regret was the wrong word to describe how they felt, maybe disappointed fit better. Every already proud parent automatically assumes that their next child will be just as healthy as the first, but that wasn't the circumstance for young Christopher. In Anthony's own words, the boy was "fucked."

Being born with Fragile X Syndrome, the plethora of effects the disorder thrust upon him were trying and horrible. Christopher's mental retardation was severe, and at that very moment, he was now forming his mashed potatoes into a pyramid after cracking open his chicken bones and sucking out the marrow.

His trademark traits being hostile and untiring hyperactive behavior, protruding bulky ears, and a comically long face. His smile had become different since he was constantly biting things and grinding his teeth. They evolved to be a bit more jagged and sharp. His mushroom haircut was something out of a 90s nightmare but he spat on the barber and tried to stab his father with a pair of trimming shears the last time he'd suggested trying a different style.

Anthony and Lisa were always looking to lay the foundation to success for their second child, just as they'd done for their first. They gave him all the tools he required to mature and move forward with stability and have a comfortable independence. But to their chagrin, Christopher's odd birth anointed conditions ensured that they would be providing his care until they were no longer capable of even caring for themselves. They'd unintentionally bit off way more than they could ever hope to chew.

"Chicken! Dead chicken!" he yelled, eagerly slamming the fractured bone onto the plate. The other family members that were seated at the table tried to ignore the ruckus, but their expressions captured subtle aggravation.

"Whoa, settle down there, buddy. You're right, it's definitely dead chicken…" Anthony said, trying to calm him but it was a task easier said than done.

Although he was not what they'd envisioned in a son, both Anthony and Lisa took on the task without complaint. They treated Christopher with the same enthusiasm and love they would have any other child. Anthony found a way to always embrace his boy through the hard times and endless outbursts.

As Anthony tried to calm him, Christopher began to unzip his pants, "Okay! Let's get you to the bathroom then!" the embarrassed father shouted.

Anthony tugged his boy away in unison with the relieved exhales from the table. When they arrived inside the restroom, Anthony opened the handicap stall and lifted the toilet seat. Christopher urinated wildly all over the bowl's rim and tile floor. He seemed to be having fun spraying his stream everywhere.

"Hey! Hey, knock it off! Cut the garbage, in the bowl, mister!"

"Papa, what's a slut?" the boy asked, still pooling his urine closer to the handle than the bowl.

Confusion overtook Anthony. As troubled as his son was, he'd never heard him use a word like that. They exited the stall after he flushed the semi-yellow contents and moved over to the sink.

"Son… where did you hear that word?"

"Papa, is Taylor a DEAD SLUT?" He moved onto the next question, clearly not capable of answering his father's counter query.

He wasn't sure where his son was getting those words from but it was concerning. Both he and his wife had tried extra hard not to contaminate his psyche and only put him around people who were respectful and conscious of the fact that their vocabulary could quickly become his. They also avoided any movies and music that offered explicit content or concepts, knowing full well that if Christopher was exposed to vulgarities, it would be like hitting a bell that you couldn't un-ring. It was an extremely challenging task, but one that he and Lisa both took seriously.

To Anthony, the bride would always be daddy's little girl, but he wasn't blind either. He wasn't some fucking oblivious idiot. The reality was there were plenty of scumbags swarming around his baby's magical celebration that had a reason to make foul remarks about his daughter. His girl was no angel, quite the opposite, in fact, but that didn't make him love her any less. Taylor was the type to play with fire until her hand was only bones. She had no issues being who she was — vocal and selfish. Her audience never impacted her actions because she simply didn't care.

There was no doubt in Anthony's mind she'd made enemies. The girl was too nonchalant about her misdeeds to avoid severing ties with those that she'd wronged. He'd seen his daughter exploit men for lavish gifts and attention with no thoughts about the future implications.

Their jealousy, obsession, and ill will had never found her before but that didn't mean they weren't lurking in the shadows. It was something he always feared. A thought that constantly jogged his mind. It was a potential powder keg for a girl who had no fear to a fault. Playing with that fire may not have destroyed her hands entirely, but it burned a lot of bridges.

Anthony knew all too well her predictable patterns and the minutiae that muddled her mind. It ran off one basic algorithm; *I'm cute and they'll want to fuck me again, so they'll eventually forgive me for whatever I do, no matter how awful I am.*

Forgive they might, forget they wouldn't. The

breed of brash, unabated immaturity that fueled her engagements was extreme enough to seat a table full of her fuck buddies right behind her own family. These weren't longtime friends that she had just happened to hook up with over the years. Either way, these were narcissistic beefcakes that were only in the picture for one reason—the hole in between her slender caramel legs.

Anthony had seen quite a few of these 'sons of bitches,' as he referred to them. He'd happened to cross paths on more than a few occasions when they were leaving her room or coming out of the bathroom half-naked before she moved into Sebastian's house. These fuckers were the tool bag specials; when they weren't drinking their protein shakes, they were busy railing his daughter and having her drink theirs. All just a few feet down the hall from him and his wife no less.

Anthony loved everything about his daughter except her selfishness and how she carried on with men. She didn't have many faults in his biased eyes, but the ones she did have dipped so deep that they were enough to make up for everything missing. The question in his mind was had she gone too far?

He knew that his daughter had ruffled many a meathead feather in her time, but he wasn't about to let some veiny, roid-raging goon ruin his daughter's special day. Anthony knew the occasion called for him to take some extra measures that would ensure his family's security and, like any good father, he had seen to that.

Anthony turned away from his son while he danced gaily and played with the motion-activated sink. He watched Christopher with a smidge of discontent on his face, knowing that the measures he was taking for Taylor would never be required for him. Maybe that was a good thing. He wasn't sure yet, but knew he would find out shortly.

He removed the revolver from his interior pocket and spun open the cylinder, confirming that six slugs sat inside. Then he closed it and shoved the gun back out of sight. He was fully prepared to handle an outburst if anyone felt so inclined to make a scene. Inside, he almost hoped that someone would try.

OVERTIME

The floor buffer was spinning on all cylinders and working in a polish to the tile that was so pristine it was a thing of beauty. The glossy sheen came into Perry's line of vision; he'd finally finished the floor. In the weathered janitor's estimation, one good turn deserved another.

From his zippered breast pocket, he extracted his best friend—his frequently filled steel flask of Wild Turkey. The stiff, supposedly "super-premium" Kentucky bourbon never let him down.

All the people he loved and looked forward to spending time around would dry up and die eventually. In fact, they all already had. The women who saw something in him would find a reason to turn their backs, but the drink would always be there waiting.

He was tired of feeling nothing day after day except for the ever-gnawing dread that served to slay the slightest hope in his skull. Even if it was a shitty feeling, at least the shock treatment he was giving his taste buds regularly throughout each boring hour made him feel something.

Perry sucked back on the medicine that made his existence bearable and gazed through the stretching windows of the conference room stone-faced. While the juice still had a funky flavor and woke him up, it didn't cause him to grimace or shudder any longer. His tolerance was on a tier where the poison couldn't normally afford him a buzz, it simply made him 'normal' again.

Through the spotless window, he noticed the hundreds of cars in the parking lot of the Biltmore and keyed in on one. The ivory white BMW M8 had 'JUST MARRIED!' painted on the back of the rear window and the classic can collection hanging from the tail end.

Sebastian's car was the type that Perry never even dreamed of sitting bitch in, let alone owning. He was born out of poverty with a limited skill set. The dimensions that hadn't already been automatically hindered by nature were busy being suffocated by the disease.

He'd caught a glimpse of the bride and groom earlier down the hallway. They both seemed so enthralled to be with each other, a feeling that he strongly doubted he'd ever be able to claim.

Must be nice having so many people that care, having each other, having any goddamn one really, Perry thought, swallowing down another Goliath gulp of both the bourbon and his own harsh reality.

The primary reason for his woes, aside from the obvious issues, was that he'd always been painfully shy. His quiet and out-of-place politeness had no place in the dog-eat-dog environment he was raised in. Growing up in the part of Yonkers that was just north of the Bronx, the color of his skin made those around him have certain expectations. Expectations that he wouldn't conform to no matter what the consequences.

Considering his lack of parental supervision, it was a bit of a miracle that he'd been able to navigate his way through the chaos and bad intentions. He didn't have luck but he always had instincts.

Perry's momma didn't really deserve the title. She was always chasing men down dark alleys or looking for the next loaded needle. Their weird relationship was more than fractured, they hadn't exchanged pleasantries in years.

As for a male role model, that concept had always been a pipe dream. Perry had never known his father but he always knew himself. He might've gotten pushed around but he never allowed himself to become what they saw him as. He'd rather have been six feet under.

Perry had never been aiming to sling dope, steal cars, or roll with self-proclaimed gangsters, but the shallowness of the streets and stereotyping of the populous left his body its fair share of bumps and bruises. Worse than the damage to his exterior was the harm to his psyche. He became even more of a recluse; the definition of a loner.

While the nasty parts of his surroundings beat him into submission, there were still parts of the street culture that he enjoyed. The musical aspects of the concrete jungle were something he related to and had always yearned to be a part of.

He was always mystified from afar when he was witness to the creative elements that arose on the boulevard. The style was charming because of its perseverance. Some people turned an evil eye to the grit but it wasn't all bad. The extreme poverty, more often than not, didn't allow them guitars, amps, and fancy drum sets, but they used what they had and created a different kind of music.

Whether it was cats rapping on the stoop, sweat-suited squads breakdancing in the park, or strangers beatboxing on the subway, the street people found a way. They made their own flavor, one that Perry had been dying to taste since the early 80s.

The only problem was, Perry wasn't prepared for the risky side of the coin that might land. In the end, the criminal element that had infiltrated the scene and style he'd worshipped, and had kept him closeted about the one thing that brought him the most joy in that dark period.

Instead of pursuing his passion, he just kept his head tucked down and remained a quiet blank canvas. The less he showed them, the less they had to hurt him with.

Once he finally escaped New York, he felt some relief being able to have his independence. It was nice not getting fucked with every time he had to step out onto the curb.

While the physical threats had been put to bed, he had a new problem now. The sheepish nature that he eventually expected to grow out of had been significantly magnified. He'd evolved into a total introvert.

As Perry continued to stare blankly at the symbol of love that was what Sebastian's jazzed-up vehicle represented, he asked himself why he didn't trust people. Inside, he already knew the answer, he'd been over it in his head a thousand times. The internal debate always ended in the same way. He wanted the answer to be different but, eventually, the truth always had to surface.

He was tired of being let down. While he'd found a way out of the city, he understood the mentality was airborne and had quickly found out it didn't exist purely where his roots were.

He found that it was just far easier to mute his interactions and avoid potentially dealing with people's rigid preconceptions altogether. Perry discovered his time in seclusion was more eventful than rolling the dice in the tricky and often stressful realm of conversation.

Speaking to women never came easy, so he mostly steered clear of it, which wasn't difficult to do. Where exactly was he supposed to meet them? When he was lugging around a mop bucket or unclogging the toilets? While he didn't want to have to deal with disappointment, a big hunk of his heart ached for companionship.

Still, Perry was happy that the nice couple had found each other because that was just who he was as a person. But another part of him envied them and wished he could find something similar. If only the stars aligned and offered him a chance.

Perry emptied out the remainder of the flask into his mouth and slipped the void container back into his maintenance suit. He shook his head left to right, trying to wake up, and looked back at the buffer.

"Well, I guess we got one more room, then we're outta here. Are you ready?" he asked, questioning the machine like it was a person. Sadly, it was probably closer to him than anything with a heartbeat.

DISCUSSING TAYLOR'S PUSSY

She liked them chiseled to perfection and stupid—the exact opposite of Sebastian. Still, there they sat with an exclusive table all to themselves, enjoying the grub while reminiscing about the warmth of her vaginal walls.

The cluster of hulking physiques stressing to conform to their suffocating formal attire looked comical arranged together in a single area. Most of the tables were designed to hold seven or eight people, but these boys were so stocked that four was the limit. It appeared as if a pack of freshly showered gym rats had arrived for leg and chest day as opposed to the celebration of a VERY close friend.

"It's pretty loose," Kwan explained.

"Yeah, after I was done with it, I stretched the shit out of it," Brick interjected.

Rocky was ripping apart the chicken with his bare hands like a savage. He ground his teeth to the bone of the carcass and sucked with his lips.

"Yeah, but everything is loose for you, lil' dick. You could be with a virgin and it'd be like sliding a hotdog down a hallway," Rocky laughed.

The fourth juice bag, Luke, started to chuckle along with Brick. He'd showered at the gym with Kwan and knew the truth behind the mockery. He wasn't sure if he was just stereotyping him or if he had cleaned up beside him too, but either way, it was funny.

"Whatever, why you looking, faggot? You just want some cock for yourself?" Kwan had a point.

"I… uhhhh, I didn't, that's just what I heard…" The most basic of comebacks appeared to be too much for him to handle.

"From who? Your mom telling stories again?" He turned the tables on him and more roaring laughter bubbled as the bunch remained ignorant to those around them.

"This is a sad day though… a real sad day, fellas," Brick said somberly.

"Why, what's wrong?" Luke was confused, an expression that frequented his face.

"Taylor's getting married."

"So? This guy is a total fuckin' nerd, what kind of dorky bitch lets the train his girl rode in on come to the after-party? Don't worry, hoss, you'll be able to hit it still, we all will, I guarantee it."

"It's not that…"

"Then what is it?" Rocky was now displaying

interest, and as he finished cleaning the bones of the pheasant, he cracked the first one, eyeing it straight down for marrow.

"I know that, I fucked her last night, stupid, but the next time I fuck her, it's gonna be adultery…"

"So?" Rocky asked, slurping out the marrow obnoxiously.

"Do you have to do that? You look like Taylor's retard brother." Kwan was not a fan of the sickening noise, it felt like nails on a chalkboard to him.

"Where do you think I got the idea?" Rocky had no shame.

"Adultery…" Brick reiterated, exhaling with a sigh, trying to redirect back to his point.

"SO WHAT? ADULTERY, ASMULTERY! WHO CARES?" Rocky set the snapped skeletal remains down having finally concluded his emulation of Christopher's actions.

"The word just sounds so… so… old. ADULTery, like an adult, you know what I mean? Are we… are we getting old?"

"Are you kidding me, guy? You're crazy! We're like a stable of well-hung stallions, fuckin' stallions, guy! Except for Kwan."

Kwan reacted to the diss perfectly and flicked a spoonful of mash that hit him square on the lips.

"You better fuckin' watch it, zipper-head! I'll fuckin' pop ya, kid!" Rocky's roid-rage was on the brink as he wiped the spuds off his mug. He could take a joke but not when he thought other people were around.

"Blow me, grease-wop!" Kwan retorted.

"It just kinda feels like we're getting old is all I'm saying," Brick chimed, reeling them back in.

"Well, a word of advice, since I've encountered this problem a few times. You know what fixes feeling old?" Brick waited for the enlightenment. "New pussy…" Rocky paused for a moment to let it sink in. "And can you guess what we're surrounded by right now?"

Brick looked up at him and smiled. His friend had done a marvelous job at cheering him up, as evidenced by his response, "Speaking of new pussy, what's your little sister's number again?"

HEY, MR. DJ

With a pair of oversized headphones half-draped over his head, DJ Buttaz scratched the record. He was playing Biz Markie's sure bet to get white folks turnt the fuck up — Just A Friend. The party was at a simmer so he was just having some fun and trying to keep himself entertained more than anything.

Ever since he was a kid, all he'd ever wanted to do was listen to music. While he didn't make a fat paycheck putting out a playlist to the masses and dropping a few tune-based puns on the mic, it was the only thing that made him tick. Feeling his fingers touch the colorful texture of the harmonies that brought life to the crowd gave him a rush.

There was a certain level of power and control that came with each gig. While the duty wasn't raking in crazy dollars, it did come with a few other benefits. Ones that if you have the right type of swagger, any hot-blooded man would be glad to capitalize on. Ones that became an addiction and had bound DJ Buttaz into the flashy drug-laced neon nightlife indefinitely. He couldn't kick the ritual now even if he wanted to.

He looked around the room of joyful people feasting and enjoying both their adult drinks and catch-up conversations. There were too many sexy chicks in the room for him to count. They were all strutting around, dolled up to the max. He was sure to score a few numbers and add some entries for his little black book.

The problem was, no matter how rounded their curves were, how model caliber their hair glistened, or how enticing their bright smiles shined, they couldn't pull his attention away from the stunning centerpiece of the wedding.

DJ Buttaz looked over at Sebastian organizing gifts near the stage. Then he quickly shifted his attention to his woman, who he needed a drool cup to be around. Taylor's enchanting brown eyes keyed in on him and a lustful leer solidified his expression.

Every time he'd seen Taylor at the clubs in the past, she was the baddest bitch in the room, but today she was just on another level. From head to toe, he wanted to lick every tiny inch of her body.

Taylor was a total party girl, and for undivine reasons, their paths seemed to cross everywhere downtown. From Club Hell to Therapy and even the nastier no-entry-fee joints like Barry's Dancefloor.

They'd screwed each other like wild animals nearly everywhere. All it took was a few purple pills and half a dozen stiff drinks. They both snapped into the same sensual mode. Their countless memorable hook-ups were some of his fondest memories.

DJ Buttaz was not a slouch with the ladies but even he felt a little special being able to tag a broad like Taylor. Considering that she was an absolute dime, he found it strange how easy she was. Either way, he sure as shit wasn't complaining.

The elongated white heels echoed against the dancefloor as she made her way over to the horny disc jockey that had left her drenched on so many prior occasions.

"You having fun yet?" Taylor asked, biting her perfectly manicured French nails.

"You know it, sexy, although, I could think of a few things that might be a little more fun than spinning wax… if you know what I mean." A cheesy grin manifested on his grill.

"Well, you might have to wait a week or two, I've got the whole honeymoon thing… but I'm sure I'll be seeing you around. You always seem to be in the right place at the right time," she said with a wink.

He watched her voluptuous ass flex with each step she took back toward her husband. Part of him was a little sullen by the thought that he'd have to wait before he got inside it again. But he also knew that great things came to those with patience.

"Fuckin' tease," he bitched to himself.

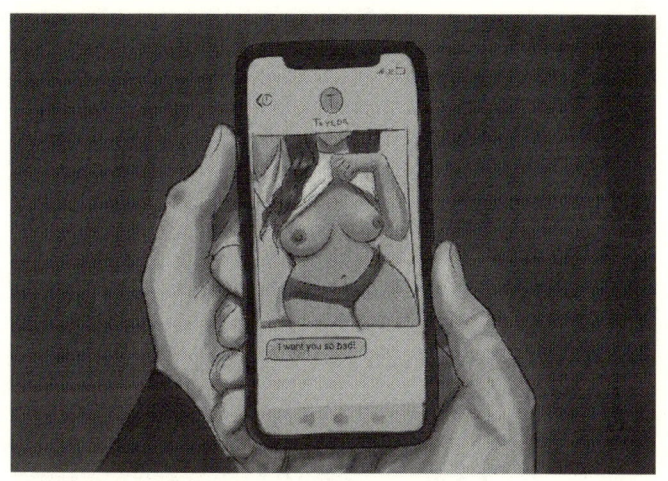

BUSINESS AND PLEASURE

Lucas poured the remainder of his third beer down after shoveling another mouthful of soggy fish into his mouth. His gut was starting to bubble a little as he shifted around in his seat, seeming more fidgety than was typical. He tried to get comfortable but the discomfort wasn't a matter of position, it seemed to be stewing inside him.

"Fish tastes kinda weird… is anyone else getting that?" Lucas asked.

"I got the chicken," Alyssa and Sarah replied in stereo. It wasn't abnormal for them; they were sort of like twins that weren't related. They both looked similar and had somehow managed to land at the same company beside both Lucas and Keith.

"Tastes okay to me, man," Keith replied, nearly polishing his plate off.

"Ugh, my stomach feels all fucked up," Lucas moaned, knowing it might just be the beginning.

"That's a shame, hope it doesn't stop you from cashing in on these free drinks," Sarah said, slurping up another swig of her rum and coke.

"This fuckin' guy? Yeah right, he drinks like every day. Nothing's gonna stop him," Keith said.

Lucas looked down at his phone for about the eleven-hundredth time. He couldn't stop reading the message over and over. Each time his eyes traced over the words, the contents of his finely pressed pants only further inflated. *I wish I was sitting on your hard cock tonight instead,* Lucas read the words while imagining Taylor's voice in his head.

He scrolled back up to the picture she'd sent before the sext. It offered an intimate glimpse of her sultry lady features. The high-definition close-up showed off her perfectly trimmed bush and enticing clit. Everything about the girl made Lucas's mouth sprout with salivation and his heart pump with forbidden lust.

Little fuckin' slut, he thought, adjusting his dick in his pants in a manner that was out of view from the rest of the table.

There were multiple snapshots that included Taylor's ass, tits, and various thongs and lingerie ensembles that he couldn't help but stare at incessantly. Suddenly, a pop-up on the phone screen censored a picture of her fingers pushing into her pussy with a note that read: "5% Battery."

"Shit, does anyone have a charger?" Lucas asked.

"Like the car?" Keith inquired confused.

"What? No, like the fuckin' cord that keeps your phone alive. What's wrong with you?"

"Yeah, cuz, we all just attend a wedding carrying cords around…" Sarah rolled her eyes.

"Speaking of weddings, Keith, have you booked your ticket to Vegas yet?" Alyssa interjected.

"You know I don't fly," he replied.

"Dude, you need to fucking sac-up already, you're telling me that you're never gonna get on an airplane EVER?" Lucas asked.

"I'm gonna be super pissed if you don't go with us. My sister comped us the fucking room, sin city, and you're not gonna party with us?" Alyssa had a secret crush on him for some time but he was a bit too dimwitted to realize it.

"You guys know I don't fucking fly, okay?"

"You know, statistically, you're far more likely to die in a car accident?" Alyssa moaned.

"You say it every time, so yes, I'm aware…"

"Who does that? Who says, I'm afraid of heights so I'm just never gonna fly? You're like the first person I know," Lucas said, racking his brain.

"John Madden didn't fly…" Keith whispered, sheepishly defending himself.

"What did you say?" Sarah asked.

"I SAID, JOHN MADDEN DIDN'T FUCKING FLY, DAMMIT!"

"Bullshit, how the fuck did he get to all those cities for Monday Night Football each week then?!" Lucas was getting fired up too.

"He took the bus…" Keith replied.

"He took the bus my ass," Lucas rebutted.

"Look it up."

"Fuck, you'd say anything to justify it."

"LOOK IT UP! USE YOUR LITTLE PHONE, BEFORE IT DIES, AND LOOK IT UP!" Keith yelled.

"Hey, forget it! We'll circle back on this. I think Sebastian is gonna say something. Looks like he's grabbing the microphone," Alyssa said, pointing up toward the stage.

Lucas's stomach suddenly started to rumble madly like a brown fountain of highly agitated feces. The sharp stomach pains meant business — he knew he needed to get to the bathroom pronto.

"Ughhh, excuse me, excuse me," Lucas bellowed, rising up from his chair and weaving his way around the girls. Wet farts that were on the verge of sharts continued to escape him as he bolted toward the restroom.

When Lucas burst inside the can, he was already speedily unbuckling his pants. He stepped through the ajar stall door and took a look at the bowl before crinkling his face in disgust.

"Fuckin' animals pissing all over the place!" he yelled as liquid started to ooze out from his rectum and saturate his underwear.

He did a Barry Sanders spin move out of the door and dropped his pants as he entered the second stall. Thankfully, that one was cleaner than the first, and it was a good thing because the watery diarrhea shot out from him just as he got over the target.

As his bare butt cheeks contacted the seating, he shivered in repulsion. He typically laid multiple sheets creating a paper barrier before he took a shit in public, but it was either raw dog the seat, or unleash the liquefied turd in his drawers.

The sloppy wave of funk invaded his nasal cavity, causing him to gag. Luckily, no one else was in the shitter to be tortured by it besides him. He kicked the door closed and twisted the handle just in case someone decided to pop in.

With an open bar, he would've expected there to be more action in the men's room but maybe it was because the groom was getting ready to speak. Those who had the ability to hold it were doing so. He pulled out the phone, wanting to review the pictures of his boss's whore wife as the soft-serve continued to gush out of his rear.

"What a fucking dunce," he grumbled, annoyed by the mere thought of Sebastian. "You think you're so smart. But if you're so smart, why is your trophy wife wrapped around my finger?" he said, zooming in on Taylor's vaginal lips.

"I already have your wife, next it'll be your job— ughhh, ughhhh!" Another violent bowel movement interrupted his nefarious thoughts and caused him to cry out. "Uggggghhhh!" he whined, sounding like a bitch version of Master P.

Just as the smell of death was drizzling out of his asshole, a visual of death manifested before his eyes, electronically anyway. Taylor's snatch vanished and his smartphone screen went black.

"I guess this means no candy crush then…" he grumbled, clenching at his belly as more of the foul brown found its way out of him.

JINXED

Sebastian took hold of the microphone and stepped over toward the front of the stage. The normally timid and soft-spoken groom was rightfully more fired up than usual. As he tapped on the mesh, a thudding sound could be heard over the PA system. "Hello? Hello? Can you guys hear me?" The crowd cheered, letting him know he was good to go.

"Can I please ask everyone to join us for a moment? I have an announcement I'd like to make. That includes the phenomenal staff who helped put this thing together. I'd like to get everyone all together at once, please. This really needs to happen with all of us together. So, everybody, just pause what you're doing and gather round."

Taylor was still smiling and seated a few feet behind Sebastian while he waited patiently as the staff filed in from the bar and kitchen prep area behind it.

"Yes, all of you, that's it, every single one. Is anyone missing from the tables?" He looked around at the tables and, at first glance, there didn't appear to be an empty seat.

"Okay, I think we're good but before I get started, there's one other person I want to join us… Jinx, can you hear me?" he asked, awaiting a response.

A tall figure stepped out from the curtain on the stage behind him. For some unknown reason, the individual was wearing a mask. The face of which portrayed an angry, bizarre, and deformed-looking jester.

A black and red ensemble covered the figure from head to toe. The upper garment was marked with a green vertically-placed evil eye sewn over the jester's torso. Tight gloves — one black and one red — matched the limp horn-like hat that curled, slumping over on each side of the mask. For some reason, the person in the costume was juggling four metallic balls of chain. They moved from belt level to being tossed high up above the mask.

The crowd seemed a bit confused by what was happening, but overall, people saw the humor and seemed to enjoy the strange and unpredictable sight. Jinx traveled down the side of the long stage, impressively maintaining balance while continuing the juggling routine.

"Ladies and gentlemen, give it up for Jinx the jester!" Sebastian yelled.

The guests applauded the creepy performer courteously, although some of the faces at the children's table looked horrified. The adults around them tried to calm and reassure the kids that the strange person was nothing to be afraid of. The event seemed quite random and not something they figured they would be seeing at such a fancy wedding.

"In case you're wondering, Jinx is here tonight for your entertainment. I've got a feeling we may need a couple of extra laughs as the evening goes on, so our jester will be helping out in that department."

Jinx let the balls drop to the carpet near the first set of exit doors. The jester applied gloved hands on the weird mask in a silly manner, like the figure was ashamed of the drop before closing the doors.

"I assure you this is a top-performing talent, as far as jesters go anyway. That's primarily because... well, being a jester really isn't a thing anymore..."

The crowd let out a chuckle, and while Sebastian continued to explain, Jinx unraveled two of the four chain balls slyly. Solid lengths of metal wrapped around the door handles and a pair of silver locks secured them.

Sebastian took out his phone and pressed the play button and circus-like music began to emanate from the speakers in the ballroom. DJ Buttaz looked confused, like he wasn't really sure how he was doing it.

"Jinx is a master motivator and also a magician of sorts. In fact, we're going to start our evening off with a little trick for you all, how does that sound?"

The crowd applauded politely while Jinx finished barricading the second and final exit. Sebastian's actions grew stranger by the minute as he began to dance by himself to the kooky music. He looked lost in his own world. One that no one else in the room seemed to have ever been privy to.

By that point, Taylor's face was plainly faking amusement even more so than earlier. She felt shots of confusion and weirdness hit her like stiff punches in the midsection. A horrible sensation began to fizz in her guts and she had no idea why. A fearful impassiveness crept up suddenly without warning as she watched Jinx stroll back to the stage.

Jinx was now dancing right beside Sebastian. They wiggled their bodies about like there was nothing off about their actions. This dragged on further for what felt like an unnecessary allotment of time as the hundreds of people watched, unsure of what exactly was going on. When the music finally died, they both froze in unison and then straightened up.

"Wow! That was quite a workout!" Sebastian exclaimed, sweat glistening on his husky cheeks.

The crowd's baffled applause still trickled in, more striving to tolerate the weirdness than actually portraying how entertained they felt. Jinx trotted over to a giant gift wrapped in jet black paper that was sitting on a dolly. The jester pushed it forward and out onto the main dancefloor until it rolled to a stop near the tables ahead of the massive chandelier. The tables that were occupied with friends and family had been arranged on the outskirts of the ballroom encompassing the dancefloor. All the focus in the room had now shifted solely to the secretive present.

"Honey?" Sebastian looked over to Taylor, who still sat radiating fakeness. "Honey, would you mind coming out to the dancefloor for a moment? I know we're not supposed to open gifts until later, but Jinx has one that warrants an early look."

Fucking idiot, what on earth is he doing? He's turning the wedding into some kind of sideshow attraction, Taylor wondered in internal ire.

Sebastian looked out to the crowd, getting them to cheer Taylor on while she smirked and marched over toward the package.

"This isn't just something for my wife either. This is actually something that is for all of us to share together on this special day. Because all of you, our friends, our family, those that have stuck by us through both the good and the bad, you ALL deserve to have a blast tonight!"

The crowd was eager for the reveal, watching Taylor closely as she carefully tore into the midnight wrapping. They were invested now because they were involved.

"Go ahead, give it a good tug, sweetie," Sebastian instructed.

As the remainder of the paper pulled free, most of it came off intact and revealed that Sebastian had a dark sense of humor. A device the likes of something most of them had seen in any number of action movies over the years sat before them. The shiny metallic exterior, huge barrels of fluid, and an array of multi-colored wires drew the majority of the room to the same unmistakable conclusion — it was a bomb.

The attendees let out their gasps in harmony, scared mumblings mixed with hopeful but still nervous laughter echoed through the beautiful ballroom. Taylor's face held firmly onto her smile. This was her special day. It had to be a prop or a gag, something like this just wasn't conceivable.

While Sebastian had never mentioned this part of the wedding, it must have just been a surprise. An eccentric surprise, but a surprise nonetheless. To her, this was all part of the trick. It wasn't possible that something like this could actually be happening to her on the day that she was supposed to get hitched.

Sebastian's family looked on, horrified. They'd known him the longest, of course, and knew better than everyone else that he didn't exactly have a rich sense of humor. His seriousness was always on short order. Everything that came out of his mouth since he'd picked up that microphone felt different. There had never been a shred of variance before, but now, somehow, his dry demeanor had evaporated. It all made the incredible circumstance that was just unveiled seem plausible to them.

How could he do this? Why? The questions raced through his father's mind as his pulse accelerated violently.

It was so hard to swallow the disturbing facts that were facing them. Even his youngest cousin, Nina, could see something was terribly wrong.

"Daddy, Sebastian is joking, isn't he?" she whispered, fearful of interrupting.

"Sure he is, let's just let him finish the trick, okay? It should all be over soon." Ivan was lying to himself but wanted to believe it so desperately. However, the performance as a whole that they'd witnessed was not the Sebastian they knew. It looked like him and sounded like him, but that was about all. It was like a disturbed mimic, as if a maniac had slipped under his skin and taken control. Either that or he'd been hiding his true colors for his entire existence.

Jinx headed back to the stage and tore the packaging off one of the other many gift boxes.

"Relax, everyone, relax, please!" Sebastian yelled over the grumblings of terror.

Sebastian extracted a small remote from his jacket and palmed it, "You see, I may have misled you all just a tad. I told you that Jinx was a magician, that's not really true, I guess by the dictionary definition anyway. However, we have performed a trick for you, that part is true. But maybe what's misleading is that the trick we're presenting is really more philosophical than visual. We've tricked you into thinking this is just entertainment." A maddening rush of laughter escaped him before he could find a way to push forward.

He straightened up again and refocused, slightly adjusting his bowtie with his fingers, then wiping his sweaty forehead with the sleeve of his tux. "Getting hot in here, good thing it's a rental." It was not a time for comedy, he quickly moved on from the dead falling joke.

"Okay, sorry, we've tricked you into believing that you'll leave this room. We've tricked you into believing that this is just another wedding. We've tricked you into believing that you're in a safe space as this pathetic society would call it."

He held up the remote and showed it to the crowd full of drooping facial features; frowns looked to be back in style.

Taylor stared at it as well. She was never usually at a loss for words, but for the first time, she thought it was better to just listen.

"This control that I hold in my sweaty hand today has the power to end our party in half of a second.

Mainly because it triggers this bad boy," he explained, pointing down toward the intimidating cluster of wires and technology.

"This sucker is comprised of enough C4 and accelerants to make this whole fuckin' block look like the next 9/11. Like a crater on the fuckin' moon, we'll all be buried."

Jinx returned to his side still appearing quite jolly and now brandishing an AK-47. The crowd was sick with fear but each onlooker was too paralyzed to speak out. They were beginning to comprehend the frightening reality; they were now at the mercy of Sebastian and his disturbed jester.

"I suggest you heed our warnings and listen very closely to my instructions. Jinx is going to take your phones now. If, for some strange reason, one of you finds a way to make a call, everybody dies. We're pretty isolated here, and I've got the entire hotel to myself. We should be alright. But I promise, right when I hear the sirens, this thing is exploding. If one of you attempts to make an escape, everybody dies. If one of you tries to interrupt our upcoming activities, everybody dies. Individually, each one of you will be asked to hand over your phone. If you refuse, Jinx will shoot you in the head. If you do not have a phone, Jinx will shoot you in the head, and shame on you for not embracing technology."

He rotated his head back and forth throughout the whole room, making eye contact with as many different individuals as he could. The nightmare was alive and well in their faces, but he still wanted to validate that his instruction was sinking in. From what he was gathering, it seemed to be effective.

"In addition to the obvious outcomes, there are a

couple more things you should keep in mind. I'm not going to lie to you anymore," he paused as a confused old woman apologized in the background.

"I'm sorry, my telephone... it's... it's at the house," she said to Jinx who held the black sack in her direction. Her words seemed to have little effect on the jester's long arms that presented the bag.

A younger woman beside her tried to explain, "She only has a landline, I swear, she's too old for a cell phone."

Jinx unloaded four rounds into her face, cutting both her life and unwanted explanation short. Two of the hot lead slugs passed through her right eyeball, one into her cheek, and the final round caught her in the throat. The kind woman's liquid contents sprayed all over the table behind her as others screeched in horror.

Jinx dropped the bag and grabbed the old woman by the back of her fragile neck. She was still stunned with the shock of watching her daughter get murdered in front of her as Jinx threw her over the table. She cried and began to hyperventilate as the wicked figure dragged down her yellowed, skid-marked panties, exposing her ass.

The others at the table stood up and backed off, their faces looked helpless. While they wanted to defend the poor old lady, it seemed they would quickly be dealt with if they attempted to intervene. The jester took the still hot tip of the machine gun and pushed it into her raunchy and weathered rectum. As the barrel plowed in as far as it could, the elderly woman's dreary sphincter skin sizzled.

"My telephone is at the house!" she shrieked as Jinx applied pressure to the trigger.

She shook and screamed like a toddler on fire. Large cherry holes wormed their way through her brittle figure, leaving her gray scalp blown clear off and her pulverized brains plastered across the room. Her innards oozed onto the tablecloth as the shots ceased. Her final act was the release of a flood of tan runny defecation that bled onto the tip of the AK-47.

Jinx then turned to a middle-aged man and put the shitty barrel into his torso. The man used his tie to wipe the vile watery feces from his phone and handed it over. Jinx snatched it and then returned to the bag.

"Okay, so one amendment, if you don't have a phone, Jinx will shoot you in the head OR sodomize you with a machine gun. So, let me just ask now, is there anyone else who doesn't have a phone? If you tell us now and save us some trouble, we'll kill you quickly, no sodomy…"

The crowd was mostly on the younger side but there were a few outliers. After a few seconds of thought, a handful of reluctant but frightened elders seemed to just want to get it over with. He saw three more hands raise. Jinx didn't wait another moment. They were all still relatively amongst the same two tables. The rest of the extended banana clip blasted off before those around them had a chance to avoid the conflict.

The sound of shattering glass and ceramic plates echoed throughout the ballroom. Slugs riddled their bodies as well as a dozen or so other people that got caught in the crossfire. Those who were still able-bodied cleared out, leaving a violent pile of dead and twitching humanity. Jinx robotically walked over and promptly put bullets in the foreheads of each tagged partygoer, then sniffed around the area for any other unintended casualties and secured their devices.

Sebastian looked on as Jinx returned to the sack and continued the morbid collection until a slender trembling hand entered into his line of sight.

"Sebastian?" the woman called out in a mouse-like manner.

Her face looked familiar but he couldn't quite place it. "I'm sorry, miss, do I know you?"

"My name is Jamie, Jamie Martin. You invited me because you donated to the City Youth Fund in support of struggling minorities."

Black tears of mascara were running down her cheeks, the thought of speaking to him was so petrifying that, while Sebastian couldn't see, she was urinating all over herself. It made sense that she chose to sit at the kid's table being that children were her profession and passion, but it also left her with a specific duty.

"Of course, Ms. Martin! How is that going by the way? Have we been seeing more opportunities so to speak?"

The strange interest in the program caught her off guard but she responded with what she believed he wanted to hear. "Yes, your generous donation has helped us achieve some wonderful things for children in the community."

"Excellent! Well, I can assure you we're going to achieve some wonderful things here today too, Ms. Martin."

"Yes, sir, but these... these children are all too young to have phones. I beg you, please believe me and spare them. They're all here at this same table with me, you can plainly see that they're harmless. I can watch them all, and I promise you they will fall in line and stay out of your way."

He stared at her momentarily before unleashing a smile, "Of course they are. Did you think they were included in this? That's definitely not the case, I may be a monster but I have other plans for the children, rest assured…"

Sebastian redirected his gaze to Jinx, who was making serious progress. There were a few bumps in the road. A few other executions had occurred as background fodder during their exchange, but the phones were piling up finally.

"Now, where was I? Oh, of course. I'm not going to lie to you anymore. The majority of us will perish today, most likely myself included, but there is a slight hope still that you should all be aware of. I will potentially be allowing a handful of folks to walk away from this. A small exclusive group that will live to speak about my wedding day massacre. A massacre that will make the most horrific spree killers, serial slayers, mass shooters, and terrorists that you see so frequently glorified in the headlines pale in comparison. Make no mistake, that's all just a drop in the bucket of blood we're filling up today," he said, pointing to the dead folks Jinx had just offed.

The crowd's nerves caused the volume of chatter laced with fright to elevate even further.

"Hey, now calm down, calm down I fucking said! In fact, don't say another goddamn word!"

Those seated quickly obeyed.

"Don't you see? You're all gonna be a part of history. Did you not hear me? And for those that didn't aim to make history today, again, let me remind you, we need at the very least one person to tell the story of what's about to transpire here today. Let that serve as your motivation. It's not the best odds, but it's far easier than winning the lottery…"

The overall shock stemming from the audience was powerful. Now that his speech had wrapped up, cries began to saturate the background chatter and petrified whispers flourished. The feeling in the air was like a death row inmate just before the last meal.

Zander could hold his tongue no longer, regardless of the risk communication posed. The family had been overwhelmed and frozen in dismay watching all the carnage that had already unfolded. They begged him to stay quiet and not draw attention to himself or any of them. The lunacy in their loved one was something that seemed far too unpredictable to call out about.

Sebastian's father felt otherwise and found the courage inside himself to stand up from his seat. The person before him was not the man he'd raised. This was not the little boy he played baseball with at the park or taught to swim at the beach. He was a demon. A demon from the bowels of the inferno that had crawled its way out and found a host in his boy.

"Sebastian! What are you doing?! This isn't you! You must stop this insanity!" Zander cried.

Sebastian shot a fuming glare toward his old man, "Shut up! You ain't the one running the show anymore! No one is running this show except me now! So, you will listen and you will obey, or, just like everyone else, you will suffer the irrefutable consequences!"

"Please, Sebastian, I beg you. Think about this more before you do other things you regret."

"Dad... you just don't get it, do you? I've invited you here today as a favor, to bear witness to my greatest accomplishment. To witness history. Yet, instead of being grateful, you insult me?! This is all... this is all just some kind of joke to you?!" The disbelief in Sebastian's words was genuine, anger forced his jaws to tighten.

"Have you gone mad?! This is not you, my son, please, this isn't you, Sebastian!"

Sebastian immediately approached Jinx, who was still collecting electronics, and handed the control and microphone over in exchange for the AK.

"That's where you're wrong, Pop. I guess the truth of the matter is... you just never really knew me," he replied, hoisting up the heavy firearm and taking aim.

Zander's eyes widened in horror, but before he could make another plea, Sebastian opened fire. A slew of shells left the tip of the AK-47, hitting him in the nose and between the eyes. The nasal cavity collapsed into his skull's interior, leaving the jaw flanking outward as the powerful shots catapulted him backwards. Blood and mind matter littered the wall behind his target and Zander landed atop the pile of mush that previously made up his cranium.

The screams and cries in the room quickly cranked to a deafening pitch. The repulsed looks on the face of his family blended with betrayal as Sebastian swapped weaponry with his partner once again. He held the controller up again, readying himself.

"If everyone doesn't shut the fuck up now, this thing is over! I literally just killed the man whose balls I came out of! Let that serve as a powerful lesson to you, my mind is strong and unflappable. My capability is unending, we are entering into an environment with no boundaries." His ramblings seemed to muffle the noise with ease. There was nothing they could do but listen and pray.

Taylor stood shaking a short distance away and realizing her worst nightmare had now become a sick hellish reality: HER WEDDING DAY WAS RUINED!

After digesting the difficult and hideous truth, she moved onto fearing for her life. Sebastian had clearly gone crackers, creating such an elaborate event. He'd mutated all of her friends and family into a school of helpless fish swimming aimlessly in his proverbial barrel.

As she pictured them all drowning in a whirlpool of violence, she watched Sebastian approach the stage. He eyed another massive gift box that towered over him so high that it looked out of place. The groom pulled away a clever paper veil and revealed another horror.

Underneath, fixed to the floor, sat a brand-new fear for the onlookers. A tall clear dunk tank like you might see at a carnival with a few steel steps and a locking metal cage. While the tank was nearly identical, the cage was unusual. Also, the fluid resting still inside the tank was not normal water. The fluid was a lighter shade of emerald green and had an ominous steam rising off the top of it.

Lugging the bag full of communication devices, Jinx approached Sebastian, who pressed and held down on the target to the right of the contraption. The seat suspended above it contorted, opening a path down to the threatening fluid contained in the tank. Jinx dropped the sack of phones through the hole and they both watched the liquid begin to fizz and bubble aggressively.

Sebastian looked at the crowd, "It's nitric acid, which I was sadly surprised to find out is clear. So, we just put a shitload of green food coloring inside to make it look cool like this. Am I the only one that thinks acid should always be green?"

The room remained silent.

He made a shooting gesture toward the crowd and lifted up the AK-47, pointing it at anyone and everyone. "Well, am I?!" he wailed.

A range of fear-laced mumbles of agreement suddenly cropped up and the crying started again.

"I'm just fucking around," he laughed yet still maintained his aim with a genuine beam on his face.

"I can see you all look worried, but don't worry, not yet anyway. This sucker is for later," he said, tapping the side of the creative murderous device affectionately.

Sebastian looked over to his far right at the videographer who remained a stone's throw away. The man had continued filming the entire sequence in fear, unsure if pressing the stop button on his camera would make him a casualty.

"Shit, that's right. Mr. Video Guy, while I sincerely appreciate your services, I'm afraid they're no longer required."

The videographer watched through the lens as Sebastian targeted the tip of the AK directly at him. He understood running made no difference and just did what he was born to do — film.

Sebastian's first bullet could have won him a marksman competition. It traveled directly through the lens of the video camera and exited through the looking hole into the videographer's head. His outdated ponytail whipped up in the air like a horse swatting flies from its ass as the contents of his skull migrated to the floor behind him.

More gasps of dread and muted tears gave way. Sebastian turned back to the crowd and tried to comfort them.

"You don't understand, I did that for all of you. If this whole thing is being recorded, then we don't need anyone to survive and tell the story, right? But I don't want technology telling my tale. I want whoever makes it out of this to have to think about what's happening here today. I want it to hurt when they rehash the hell I'm about to unleash."

Taylor stood frozen and utterly chilled to the bone. For the duration of their association, Taylor had always believed she was the one reeling in the trophy catch, but her view was distorted. Sebastian didn't look or act like a fisherman but he'd had his line in the water the entire time.

He was homicidal, he was suicidal, he was sick-minded, and maybe most concerning of all, he was unconditionally bloodthirsty. Maybe the scariest part of what was transpiring was that it didn't seem to matter who got splattered judging from his most recent victims.

"Now that the camera guy is dead and Jinx has collected all of your phones for good measure, I'm going to remind you again, remember the rules. If you somehow make a call, the cops would be a waste. They can't save you from today's destiny, only you can save yourself. You made the choice when you accepted our wedding invitation... you chose your own fate."

Sebastian let the weapon relax at his side for a moment and kept his gaze on the crowd.

"Also, I think it's important to display my competence to you. I don't want anyone to think I haven't planned accordingly. I think that a short demonstration can help me build confidence in all of you and, that way, you'll know just what the fuck we're into right now."

He stepped over past the bulky metal device still looking out at the crowd before removing the remote from his pocket. He pointed it square at an old lady he'd never met before.

"Something old..." he switched his aim of the remote to a crying toddler at the designated kid's table, "something new..." Next, he switched his aim to the slack-jawed DJ Buttaz and his colorful equipment. "Something borrowed..." he paused for a moment, adding one final artful and overly-dramatic effect, "something... BLEW!"

Just as he pressed the button on his remote, he turned back to the whiney children's area where Jamie Martin was still seated, ever-protective of the young. The audience soon realized that he wasn't bluffing, his display proved him fully proficient in the construction of bombs.

The sick play on words came to life as the children's table exploded and caught fire. The young had come undone; their tiny sizzling parts quickly blackened as they launched in a multitude of directions.

Their once internal juices had been freed to paint those around them with copious amounts of hot extract and an assortment of other meat and organs. The random limbs and still quivering stumps jiggled about as the audience watched in horror. The blast assured that the children would cry no more, Sebastian had seen to that.

Was it possible that, for Jamie's self-sacrifice and general willingness to accommodate, Sebastian had given her a quick and easy way out of the event? Taylor couldn't be sure as she stared at the ghastly stub shooting off blood like a fancy sprinkler system where the innocent woman's legs previously sat. Jamie's dress was tattered and she looked like a ragamuffin. Her once beautiful face was now sliding off her skull and one of her elbows had been left exposed down to the bone.

"You son-of-a-bitch! My baby! Ricky!" a woman screamed rising from her chair and rushing into the still smoldering chaos. Her husband tugged reluctantly on her arm before letting it go; she was far braver than he was.

While young Ricky had been blown into bits, his mother dove beside him trying to scoop what was left of his tiny body into a single unit.

"Jinx!" Sebastian yelled with a look of discontent.

The twisted jester raised the rifle and squeezed the trigger. The burst tore her body to pieces until she lost movement and became an extension of the pile of gore.

"Now everyone be fucking quiet! You're not bringing them back with your tears! But if you want to join them, well, feel free…" Sebastian's stern yet dark tone commanded them.

He was playing the hard-ass, but inside, he was all Jell-O at the moment. A warm fuzzy feeling poked throughout his intestines and elevated his brain to a temporary high as he came to the realization that he'd finally broken them.

He didn't believe it would happen so quickly but he was glad to be ahead of schedule. He'd shown his hand; they were all just meat to him. It didn't matter if they were family, a stranger, or a child, they would all die just the same.

There were no limits anymore or emotions attached and no predictable outcome. He held the reins of his human horses and remained in complete control as the voices in the room settled with the smoke from the detonation.

The panic and chaos that Sebastian had created was unequivocally legitimate. It was now apparent to the guests that they'd be taking part in an event that was terrifyingly unique. A blasphemous, sadistic, and terminal celebration. A display of utter horror that was unavoidable and uncontrollable.

They'd all arrived physically hours ago but were just now arriving mentally. The initial pretense was false; today was no ordinary autumn wedding day. For most of them, today would be both their first and last… wedding day massacre.

BATHROOM BREAK

The weirdo jester entered the restroom brandishing the AK-47 ready to kill. The clownish figure checked out the pair of urinals that sat stinking right beside the entrance, then stepped inside the first stall and gazed upon the foul piss-stained porcelain. Finally, the creep worked down to the last stall and pushed the closed door open with the barrel of the machine gun. It was also empty.

Once Jinx had cleared the entire commode, the deranged entertainer approached the exit. But just before leaving, a closed janitorial closet crossed Jinx's line of vision. A thought ran through the trickster's mind as the gloved hand reached for the chrome doorknob.

Upon realizing it wouldn't turn, the AK erupted, blowing the handle clean off the door. As the steel door squealed open, the closet was revealed, and just like the rest of the room, it was completely empty.

Jinx examined it thoroughly but found nothing of importance. Just a handful of cleaning products, a stockpile of toilet tissue, paper towels, and a nasty mop simmering in a bucket of stagnant gray water.

***

The gunshots were so loud that Lucas wished he could've covered his ears. Instead, he laid frozen in terror trying not to allow his gut to be triggered again. Sweating profusely, he was contorted in an awkward position. Fitting himself into the wooden cabinet below the sink was anything but easy or comfortable, but nonetheless, he'd found a way to stuff himself inside.

A soap refill cap was lodged halfway up his ass and some of the spare rolls of toilet paper were digging into his torso awkwardly. He listened to the beautiful sound of the bathroom door opening back up again, and the ominous footsteps of the murderer that had stalked the area moments ago make their way out.

He'd been stuffed in there for some time. Lucas had been able to hear Sebastian's entire "speech" while inside. It took him hearing the first shots before he truly grasped what was going on out there.

The forthcoming explosions, screaming, and general panic amongst the tormented guests told him everything he needed to know. He knew it was only a matter of time before they took a gander inside the bathroom. Thankfully, Lucas was able to get creative and it saved his shitty little ass.

"Fuck, Jesus, fuck," Lucas mumbled to himself, still not sure if he was ready to leave the confines of the cabinet.

"What do I do now?" he whispered to himself.

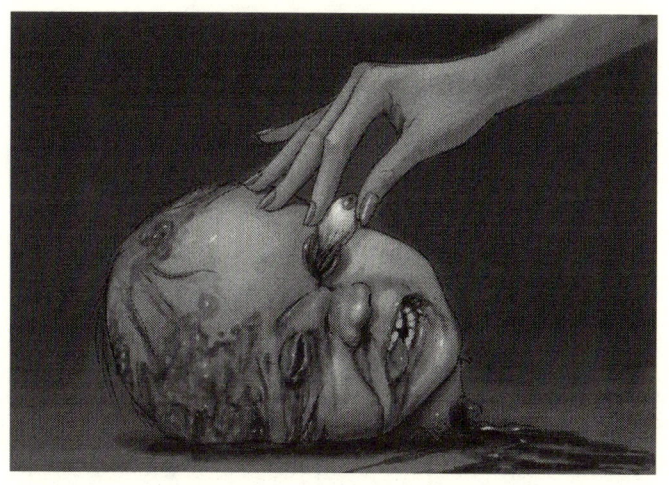

SLOPPY SECONDS

Jinx was just returning after conducting a thorough search that included the rest of the hotel and parking lot. During his absence, Sebastian had continued entertaining his guests as best he could.

The jester came through the doors with the barrel of the AK square against the neck of the hotel manager who looked about ready to shit a brick. A few other new faces surrounded him. The foursome of weeping maids and Perry Jackson, the wide-eyed maintenance man, rounded out the rest of the pack.

Perry had just come in to fix a few light fixtures and wax the floors in the conference rooms. It was supposed to be his day off. He was supposed to be lazing about the house but ownership wanted him to wrap up a few more things in preparation for the Biltmore's grand reopening.

Picked the wrong fuckin' day to clock some OT, he thought as they continued forward. Suddenly being thrust into such an absurd conundrum almost didn't surprise him anymore. As far back as he could remember, he'd always had shit luck.

"Few stragglers, huh? Please, come on in and join the party." Sebastian turned back to the crowd as Jinx secured the door again.

Sweet Jesus, what the hell happened in here?! Perry's brain wondered hysterically as he took notice of the violence and bloodshed that was sprinkled about the massive room. He was in no position to do anything drastic, but upon assessing the situation, he got an immediate guttural hunch that his best approach would be to blend in.

As Jinx trotted off back toward the stage and Sebastian remained focused on the crowd, Perry did his best to camouflage in with the actual guests. While the flock of shaken and sickened Biltmore employees remained standing frozen in place, he slyly slid into a chair at one of the tables beside him.

He felt the damp inner contents of the woman who'd been blown away by Jinx just a short time earlier assimilate into his rear. The janitorial outfit stuck out like a sore thumb, but being seated kept him somewhat detached from the other staff.

"So, most of you have just finished up your meals, what's the verdict on the scampi and baked cod? Did catering pass the test?"

No one responded.

"C'mon, don't be afraid, I'm not just gonna freak out!" Sebastian shook his head about like a rock star releasing a weird giggle. It was clear his reality was merging with his madness. His behavior was out of control but his audience could do nothing but hang on his every word.

"Do we have any vegetarians here today? Sorry, you know, I literally just realized we didn't have a vegetarian option on the menu… can you sense my sarcasm?"

A grave sincerity suddenly took hold of him. "Well, if you can't, allow me to lay it out for you. I don't give a good fuck if you're one of those assholes that's been flaunting your 'I love my farmer' bumper sticker in my face in traffic every day, or if you've been eating off the dollar menu for a decade. That's because today you're gonna be consuming a meal that's… well, unimaginable really. But that's the great thing about what we're doing here today. There are no limits."

Cindy sat nervously beside Paula, her foot rocking up and down incessantly as Sebastian moved closer to their table. His eyes grazed over them gradually in a perverted manner. They could only hope that he wouldn't mention them in a room with so many other options.

"So, I hope all of you left some extra room today because your life may very well depend on it." He turned back to his shaken wife, Taylor, who was still standing confounded in the same spot that she was before he'd killed most of the children.

"Honey, can you please go clear off the long table? The one with the gifts? You can just put them on the stage with the others and, oh, put a couple of chairs there too please."

Taylor did as her nut-bag husband instructed, while he did exactly what her friends had feared most: spoke to them.

"Taylor! Taylor! I want a gift! Pleaaaaaasssssseee!" Christopher looked back at his father. "I want the gift even more than the ice cream, Papa! Please, just one and I promise to be the best boy!" he screamed.

Anthony had done an almost miraculous job of keeping his special needs son muzzled throughout Sebastian's ramblings but the boy was overflowing with energy. It wasn't often that Christopher had to be on his best behavior, but if there was any day to keep a low profile, it was that day.

Anthony was constantly whispering promises of froyo into his son's ear to keep him as distracted from the melee as possible. Froyo was his favorite thing in the world and Anthony often used the concept of the delicious dessert almost like you would a treat to a dog.

"You could get both today, the caramel and the chocolate sauce, whip cream, sprinkles, and even gummies too. But you have to stay quiet for me, we can go every day this month, okay?" he whispered into Christopher's humungous ear.

Up to that point, it had been working just fine, dangling the thought of receiving his favorite treat each day had really hit home until he saw the gifts. Christopher loved destroying paper (or anything really) and revealing what was beneath. Just the thought of finding out the contents excited him.

Anthony again tried to hush his boy as best he could but he'd attracted his psychotic son-in-law's attention. Sebastian shifted a glare over at them as Jinx walked toward their table, gently clenching the AK. Christopher looked up at the wrinkled mask with the forced smile impressed upon it,

"Do you wanna play cards with me? We could

play Go Fish! Or War! Or… even Old Maid!" he asked sincerely.

"Dad… I've only got one of you left now," Sebastian explained, pointing back to his birth father's splattered remains, "but if you don't simmer the fuckin' sped down, it'll get a lot worse than me just becoming fatherless, understand?"

Anthony gritted his teeth and clasped his hand over his son's mouth. A ball of stress formed around his tight sternum; the rage prodded him to consider whipping out the gun and putting a hot one right between his eyes but the fantasy was just that.

He had the means but was clearly outnumbered. He knew any rash action could still potentially spell doom for everyone. What if he missed? How would the murderous jester respond? Would the bomb still somehow go off? There were too many variables to make a move out of pure emotion.

He'd been calculating it the entire time. There were a couple of moments they'd had their backs turned to him already, but the uncertainty of the situation still hadn't given him any confidence. He couldn't be sure that he wouldn't end up killing everyone if he took a shot at playing the hero. If or when he did make a move, it had to be at the perfect moment. If it wasn't precise and premeditated, that would be the end without question.

"Very good," Sebastian said, appearing satisfied with the sight of the muted boy fidgeting in his father's arms. He turned his attention back to the girls at the table, their trembles resembled a pair of junkies going through crank withdrawals.

"Cindy, gosh, it's good to see you here. I heard you were a little under the weather today but I'm glad you toughed it out. I'm sure you'll be happy you did by the end of it. By the way, who did you come to the wedding with?" Sebastian held the microphone to her lips and awaited a response. She looked over to Paula whose eyes screamed DON'T YOU DARE FUCKING SAY IT!

"I… I… came with Paula!" she finally confessed, pointing her finger across the table.

"You bitch!" Paula screamed, unhappy with her failure to omit her from the conversation.

"You're the one that dragged me here today! It's your fault we're in this mess!" Cindy's vindictive perspective was now so rigid that it had been crystalized. The rest of the way they were joined at the hip; in the shit together. Whether Paula liked it or not.

"Ladies, ladies, whoa. Please, there's no need to get so upset. The fact that you are such great friends that two of my lovely wife's bridesmaids would take each other to a wedding… while maybe to everyone else it's a little strange but, to me, that's perfect really. Because now, Cindy, I'm going to give you a chance to save your good friend's life. Why don't the two of you walk up to the table over there where my sweetheart is?"

"Please, Sebastian…" Cindy begged.

"It would serve you best to do exactly as I say. I can get a little aggravated when I repeat myself."

They both walked over to Taylor without a fight, knowing persistence wouldn't do them any favors. There was no way to reason with a madman.

Next, he looked over to the hotel and wedding staff that were huddled in the corner of the room like a pack of terrified chickens.

"Again, I just want to thank this unbelievable staff for doing such a phenomenal job today." He put the remote into his jacket so he could clap his hands, "Really, let's all give it up for them."

Most of the guests were out of it. They sat crying silently or too fear-stricken for enthusiasm.

"Fucking clap! BEFORE I CUT SOMEONE'S GODDAMN HEAD OFF!" Sebastian yelled, feeling they weren't recognizing the team enough.

The bizarre applause became thunderous, there was even a couple of whistles in there as he began to motion to the group.

"I'm gonna need all of you to join us up at the table too, please," Sebastian explained to the group.

No one seemed to be ready to follow instructions, the group was so gravely disturbed that they all sort of looked at each other instead of following the request.

"Are you deaf? Everyone standing, get your asses up here now before I really get upset..." he grumbled.

While the thirty or so staff reluctantly trudged behind Sebastian, Perry remained seated, hoping that the other random guests he was seated around kept their mouths shut. He doubted anyone would want to communicate with the madman on the microphone, but to his experience, there was always one asshole.

The group remained silent to his relief while the staff made their way back to the side of the stage area where the long table sat.

Sebastian pointed to a seat at the right side of the table, "Cindy, you can have a seat here," the tone of his voice indicated that he was still thinking while

75

scanning through the horde of help.

His vision settled on a petite waitress that was shaking wildly and whose mascara was racing down her face.

"Jesus, you look like a raccoon right now, tell us your name, please?" he asked, nearly touching her lips with the microphone.

"J—Jasmine," the girl said like she was now on autopilot. She was gripped by a tremendous dread and did exactly as she was told.

"Well, it appears that you're gonna be the representative for the staff. Go ahead and take a seat right here beside Cindy," he said, patting the table.

Jinx approached Sebastian with a small circular wrapped package and offered it to him. "Really? You got this for me, buddy? Wow, you shouldn't have." Jinx mimed actions, prodding him to open it.

As Sebastian quickly finishing tearing through it, Jinx set another much larger rectangular box at his feet. The rest of the heart-peppered paper fell to the floor and Sebastian looked a little confused by the massive length of orange extension cord that he was suddenly holding.

"I'm not sure I understand…" he mumbled.

Jinx now motioned toward the bigger box that sat under him. The overly acted confused grimaces morphed into a mischievous smirk. It was clear they knew where they were going with this but did their best to put on a show for the group.

The loftier oblong container, to the horror of those seated (and even more so to the ones who were standing), revealed a brand-new 18-inch electric chainsaw. Jinx took one end of the extension cord and plugged it into the socket.

"Wonderful..." Sebastian whispered to himself.

"Honey? Can you go fetch me a couple of those dead kids, please?"

Jinx finished removing all of the wrapping and activating the saw for use as Sebastian's command echoed throughout the tall ceiling of the ballroom. Sebastian clipped the microphone to the stand in front of him and retrieved the detonator from his pocket. He handed it over to Jinx and took hold of his first gift.

"What? What do you mean?" Taylor asked.

She knew damn well what he meant. She didn't want to touch the dead but was quickly motivated to complete the task. It only took Sebastian choking down on the handle of the chainsaw for a few pulls. When the cycling meat-ripper began to make its way toward her, the decision became instinctual. Being grossed out made more sense than becoming the gross out.

She didn't take much thought in her selection, she just grabbed hold of the two bodies that were closest to her. She found the wrists of two young boys and pinned them together, wrapping both of her hands around them. The pair seemed to be in the age range of seven to ten years old, they barely understood what life was about and it had already been taken from them.

The first one looked like he was of Italian descent and had a large piece of metal (presumably from the device that had been hidden under the table) driven into his forehead. It was causing his still warm flesh to leave behind a wide blood trail on the floor as she hauled them closer to the stage. She'd kicked off her shoes just prior but the footing was not ideal.

Taylor tried not to look at them but couldn't help it. She suddenly realized that she was dragging the lifeless shell of her younger cousin, Michael, and the still twitching body of his next-door neighbor and best friend, Joshua.

She had babysat the pair of them a handful of times back in her teenage years. While they'd always found a way to get on her nerves, each time she always admired their relationship. The two held an unbreakable bond in life that, in a gloomy irony, had now transferred over in death.

Joshua was the only black student in the school district and hadn't made friends easily. Michael had never seen a difference between them and always had his friend's back. For their age, they were surprisingly intellectual or at least they had been…

Joshua's left leg was mutilated from the thigh down. A clutter of violence glistened upon him that didn't remotely resemble a limb. It dangled, barely attached but somehow still holding by a string of rubbery skin. The boy's vivid and ghastly post-mortem state forced Taylor's body into a moment of unintentional hesitation.

She began to throw up a disgusting mixture of still-bubbly champagne and undigested fish. She had aimed for the floor but much of it inadvertently landed all over young Joshua's dead face. It was still dripping out of her mouth and nose when Sebastian began to chastise her.

"We don't have all fucking day here! If that's making you sick, then I'm not really sure how you're gonna make it through the rest of this."

Taylor straightened up, finding a way to power through her emotions and dragged both of the dead children through the puddle of her vomit before setting the corpses at the feet of her husband.

"Thank you, my darling," he said, revving the chainsaw toward her again. She tried to step away from his madness as Sebastian's playful swipe of the rotating blade only missed her ear by a few inches. His action bullied Taylor backwards, causing her to stumble and fall on her ass.

Anthony again gritted his teeth watching from his table. The lunatic was toying with his little girl and it took everything for him not to pull out the gun and start firing. But he knew the right moment hadn't arrived yet. The demonic jester was still angled toward him. Jinx's wicked midnight mass-manufactured eyes could have been looking at anyone in the room, but Anthony felt like they were staring a hole through him. So, he remained still, holding onto Christopher as best he could.

Sebastian looked down at the two dead boys and then back over to Cindy, "Well, at least it's already cooked for you. So, what'll it be, white or dark meat?" he asked her in all seriousness.

Cindy mouthed responses unintentionally. There was no volume to anything she was trying to say, her speech was going through confused motions. She could only wonder what he had in mind for them next...

"No preference, I guess? It's all the same to me too," Sebastian agreed.

He shrugged his shoulders and slammed the spinning metal chain into Michael's neck first. It tore through the adolescent tissue and spine in seconds and sparked against the floor. A flood of hot red showered outward, splattering the white shirt that

79

laid under Sebastian's tux. Some erupted with such force that the splatter arch reached the gorgeous gown of his bride who sat in horror just a few feet away. More cries and moans crept up in the peanut gallery but there was nothing they could do other than watch the carnage unfold.

He set the decapitated head on the table in front of Jasmine, forcing her to cover her eyes as the vacant baby stared back at her. He pulled the large hunk of wreckage that had killed him from the depths of his forehead and eye socket, then tossed it on the floor.

Sebastian examined the boy's eye which was now dangling out of the socket but still intact. "Should be fine still," he mumbled to himself.

He returned his gaze to Jasmine, "Don't want you breaking a tooth now," Sebastian remarked before turning his attention to the other body.

He sawed through Joshua's throat with equal efficiency. Sebastian then lifted the second boy's head off the puddles of bodily fluid, void of remorse and conscience. He balanced the second skull to stare at Cindy, by now the pure embodiment of a hysterical mess. Sebastian set the gnarly gore-drenched saw onto the ground and retrieved a bucket from beneath the table.

"Paula, and all members of the fantastic Biltmore staff, please join me on the dancefloor," Sebastian asked politely.

They all followed behind him in line like cows at the slaughterhouse. Sebastian continued toward the middle area of the floor, carrying the bucket at his side. Jinx trailed the group, keeping a close tail while the jester's gloved thumb rubbed around in a circular pattern atop the detonator.

"Form a ring please, one nice big circle that you can all fit into," Sebastian instructed, twirling his finger about.

As Paula began to integrate herself in with the staff, Sebastian grabbed hold of her arm firmly. "Wait," he whispered.

Once they had all appeased Sebastian's wishes, he reached into the bucket and grabbed hold of a cluster of silver handcuffs. He slipped the first pair onto Paula's wrists and fastened them to a point of pinching discomfort.

"Get in the middle, bitch."

She slid inside, penetrating the large circle, and stood directly in the center just as she was told. Sebastian nodded and slapped the next set onto the left forearm of the glossy-eyed girl who stood in front of him. While she wasn't happy with her new accessory, she wasn't prepared to argue. Sebastian stretched the unlocked cuff to the large burly gentleman beside her. The cook, still wearing his ridiculous chef hat for some reason, discordantly jerked his arm away from him.

"You're not putting that fucking thing on me! I'm not playing this sick game anymore."

"Very well."

Before Sebastian finished snapping his fingers, the chef's silly hat had flown away, along with the top of his head. Splintered bone and brains splashed over the woman beside him, getting in her mouth and covering most of her face.

"Don't anyone move a fucking inch! Is it really too much to ask? Just follow my simple instructions or else!" Sebastian yelled.

Many in the group jumped but, ultimately, they still stood their ground. They knew that any false move could potentially be their last. She wiped the man's warm interior off of her nose and out of her eyes and hair as best she could. Jinx kept the still smoking AK fixed on the circle of staff. The jester's red gloved finger now sat resting on the trigger.

"So, let me just ask now since we have assholes that want to impede on what's inevitably going to happen here anyway, is there anyone else who doesn't want to play? Anyone?! Speak now, or forever hold your peace!"

You could've heard a pin drop as he fastened the rest of the cuffs until the entire staff had become one; strung together by the resilient metallic linkage. The cook's rude delay prompted him to secure the remainder of the restraints even tighter than Paula's. Most of their hands had already transitioned to a purple or blue shade.

"Alright, I think we're ready to get started now."

Sebastian approached the microphone near the table again, then turned back to look at the duo of depressed guests. As he did, Jinx approached him with a small clip microphone and pinned it to the top of his tux.

"Hello, hello? Can you guys still hear me?" he asked, stepping away from the standing mic that Jinx had set off to the side. "Check one, check one, am I good to go?"

Jinx nodded the evil mask and gave a double thumbs up. The jester's facial covering didn't allow for any of the creepy figure's inner emotions to be revealed, but the sinister entertainer's body language seemed quite joyful.

"Sorry, the sound can be a little tricky sometimes. Okay, I'm sure you're wondering what this is all about. This is quite the extravagant setup we have, now what could we possibly be doing here? I know you were all probably a little bored watching us scramble around and get our shit together, but trust me, the wait, the setup... it's all gonna be worth it."

Taylor stared at her little cousin's destroyed head sitting atop the table still waiting to wake up. It was all a blurry dream — a horrible, cruel, and unusual nightmare. It had to be. What was unfolding before her couldn't possibly be how her life was set to play out. She had so many other ideas and selfish goals.

"I don't know about you, but I'm a sucker for tradition. And while I do strongly respect age-old customs, I think it's also important to build our own. Times change, right? So, I wanted to do something that's a little more relevant. Something that is going to take some fucking nuts to repeat. That's what today's about. Today, we craft a blueprint for the future."

Sebastian raised his hands high above his head, "Today, we partake in some groundbreaking and innovative behaviors that will undoubtedly be mimicked at some point in the future. What we'll be involved in is a massacre, but on a granular level, when you break it all down, it's far worse. They'll probably need to create a new term for it, really."

"I'm not sure about you, but when I think of the word massacre, I think of a profound number of casualties. BODIES EVERYWHERE. Let the bodies hit the floor! Let the bodies hit the floor!"

Sebastian looked over to Jinx as they both threw up the devil horns and the jester began to headbang.

"Remember that song? Lead singer actually died of a heart attack, would you believe that? No? Well, you can believe this, 99.9% of you will be wishing you could've gotten off that easy when your turn comes around." A perverse smile scurried across his face.

"You see, in a normal massacre, the deaths are usually quick, be it by a bomb's blast or rapid gunfire. The goal of any mass murderer typically is to take out as many people as he or she can, and to do so as quickly as fucking possible. It's all about the numbers usually…" Sebastian's left hand fidgeted about at his side before he began to spasm and rapidly tap his leg.

"See that method just… it leaves the artist so restricted, handcuffed really… no pun intended. There's no time to enjoy nor admire the work you're doing. It's literally about fifteen or twenty minutes of pure gory orgasm before you're inevitably captured or forced to suicide. Something about it has just always felt all wrong to me." His furrowed brow showed this wasn't just part of the show, it was something he'd thought about for quite some time.

"So, I asked myself, what other options do I have? I could become that classic, closeted serial killer. The one that picks people off one or two at a time over the course of a few decades and maybe, just maybe, if I'm extraordinarily prepared, careful, and a little lucky too, I can avoid detection. Again, something about that just doesn't seem right or fair. More so especially these days. We live in a very instant society. This approach might have worked years ago but now we're conditioned. We want everything now; we *need* everything now. Plus, who wants to look over their shoulder every day and worry about being caught each morning they wake up? Not me. Am I right?"

The entire crowd remained dumbfounded. The questions were all rhetorical but they couldn't have answered them even if they wanted to.

"So, to me, the puzzle became how could I have both right now? The artistic freedom and intimacy that accompanies a well-plotted single slaying and the sheer numbers that are a given when committing a mass murder. The answer is actually much simpler than you'd think. It just takes an extra touch of patience, which most people in my position don't tend to come equipped with."

"How is it possible, you ask? Easy, find a large group of unsuspecting people who trust you, and show everyone that you're in complete control. What better event to use as a mirage than one which everyone attending believes to be the next step in life, but ironically, it's the grim end of it."

Sebastian reached beside him and pet the head of dead Michael, "Now that I'm able to take my time with each of you, this will not simply be some silly mass extermination, no, not by a long shot. Today, we set the trend. When all is said and done, this wedding day massacre will do for marriage what Columbine did for education. I hope you're all as excited as I am." Sebastian exhaled deeply and steadied his shoulders proudly as he turned his attention back to the girls.

"Now, obviously, as I stated earlier, the two of you will be competing to save your friends, at least for now… and also to advance forward and not be exposed to an agonizing punishment…"

Jinx grabbed the chainsaw and revved it up again. The jester seemed just as excited as Sebastian to be there.

"All you have to do is be the first person to eat the eyeballs and tongue out of the dead child's head in front of you."

The faces of the "competitors" were stained with their own vile interpretations of how the gruesome chore would feel. A horrible feeling of dread and impending doom moved into their bodies.

"And remember, if you don't want to play, that's fine, you can join our friend here."

Sebastian walked back over and kicked the crumpled corpse of the hero cook numerous times. He psychotically beat on the motionless body over and over. Finally stepping on the mashed brains disrespectfully for good measure.

The tension was building, the girls had no idea exactly how they were going to react once it started. Sebastian didn't give them much time to dwell on the notion or think it over.

"Okay… ready… on your mark… get set… GO!" Sebastian hollered out.

Jinx held down on the chainsaw to signal it was time for the race to begin. The clownish figure danced about like a child at the playground.

Cindy and Jasmine both looked at each other for a moment, still dazed by the concept of what they knew they needed to do. Suddenly, a simultaneous shift occurred and they both began to attack each of their respective skulls like animals.

It would have been quite easy to misjudge their character. Prior to the start, they both appeared repulsed and unwilling. But once Sebastian blew the preverbal whistle and their lives (as well as many others) were on the line, they tore into the raw flesh like it was chicken pot pie.

The still rickety waitress pressed her pointed nails into the corner of Michael's left eye socket and hooked onto the orb with ease. She tore it free after a few stiff tugs, but to her surprise, it came out relatively easily. She placed it on the table trying to hold off on the most difficult task until she'd removed the other parts that were required.

Cindy took the opposite approach, balancing the head upside down and thrusting downward with her elbow onto Joshua's jaw. The lofty pressure she exerted caused the jaw to snap back rapidly. With the mouth unhinged, she went in, giving Joshua his first and last disgusting French kiss.

She closed her top and bottom teeth toward the base of the uncharacteristically, stationary muscle and bit down as hard as she could. Gagging on the wet and gamey chunk, she could feel her teeth penetrating it, but when she tried to pull away with the muscle, she was denied.

She looked over at Jasmine who had just finished removing Michael's second eyeball and knew she needed to be quicker. She started to grind her teeth from side to side vigorously, scraping into the rubbery flesh without remorse against her enamel until it finally broke free.

Suppressing her uprising of dry heaves and controlling her hysterics, she collected as much spit as she could in her mouth. Once the tongue was essentially floating in her saliva, she took one quick massive swallow and was able to wash it down successfully. If it was an adult tongue, she probably would have choked on it, but she was fortunate that it still hadn't fully developed.

"Wow, and I thought Jinx was usually the quiet one! But that's what I call biting your tongue!" Sebastian yelled, truly relishing in the rivalry.

The onlookers remained sickened and unmoved by Sebastian's crass words. Those who stood in the circle released a burst of throat-ripping screams of encouragement. Their words made little difference, yet still they wailed. It might have been a morbid premonition but they already sounded dead.

Cindy checked back in on her competition; the poor woman was breaking down. She had the dead boy's eyes out but was struggling tremendously with the tongue. She was trying a similar tactic but wasn't strong enough to break his jaw. She picked up the head and started slamming the chin into the lip of the stage behind her.

Cindy didn't take time to pity her, laying the back of the head on the table and violently plunging her index fingers into each socket of the dead child's gushing face. Once she got herself a firm grip, she held tight and placed the skull on the floor.

She then set her heel down on the face and pulled up, ripping the first already dislodged eyeball free with ease. She set the peeper on the table and went right back to business tugging at the second one. She was able to get it loose with record timing. The sadistic surge of spontaneous savagery must have been lurking inside her but she had no time to reflect on her shocking success.

At first, Cindy utilized the same saliva-soaking method she'd used on Joshua's tongue to try and get them both down, but they were too bulky. Maybe going for the double was a mistake. She knew she was going to have to chew to make it happen.

She carefully used her tongue to roll each of the orbs between her upper and lower molars and took a deep breath. She readied herself and closed her eyes tight before her teeth started to crush down.

The normally unseen mortal juices launched out through her open mouth like her jaws had just mashed down on a cherry tomato. The disgusting filmy sauce sprayed over Joshua's motionless chin as Cindy gagged, trying to keep from throwing up. The fibrous tunic was rubbery; like a chunk of fatty chicken that the chef forgot to trim. With a more focused effort, she was at last able to power through and flatten out the marbleized mouthful.

A surge of hot vomit sprang up and she reached deep, achieving a meditative focus to avoid pitching the contents of her mouth and gut. Cindy pooled the regurgitation, her saliva, and Joshua's juices. With her jaw rattling manically, she finally swallowed.

The eyes felt even stranger than the tongue going down, she distinctly sensed the gory tip of the nerve ending tickle her esophagus as the staff begged and pleaded with her not to finish. But little did they know, she had officially sealed their fate.

Unfortunately for them, their representative still sat stress-filled and struggling. Jasmine continued thrashing Michael's head robotically in a daze of chaos. She was unaware that the event had already concluded.

Sebastian approached Cindy with a big grin that ran ear to ear, "Open your mouth, please."

She obeyed his wishes and he used his bloodstained fingers to poke around and inspect the cavity which he found to be clear.

"Okay, that's it then. The first event has now concluded!" he yelled.

Sebastian looked over to Jinx who stood solemnly and nodded. The demonic jester took hold of the already gore-clad saw and set the wet chain to cycle. The other guests looked on in horror as he began to run through the screaming circle of handcuffed help almost instantaneously.

Meat ripped, blood poured, and limbs detached with ease. They fought and jumped, trying to avoid the saw blades but it was inevitable. Jinx started at their kneecaps, taking a few stiff kicks en route to coming full-circle. With every other strike the frightened staff pointlessly threw, a limb was unmade until there was no longer a usable defense mechanism left to protect themselves with. Eventually, they would each slump down onto the ground, just like the one before them — legless and screaming.

After the first round, there was so much crimson flowing on the wooden floor that it was closer to a swimming pool than a puddle. It had become so ridiculous that it was stretching out from the dance arena and beginning to brown the rugs at the trembling feet of the seated guests in the dining area.

Many of the maimed were falling into the grips of shock and staring mindlessly up at the twinkling chandelier while their extremities shuddered from the fresh separation. It looked like enough legs had been harvested to build a human centipede.

The rest let uncontrollable wails of agony echo as they writhed atop the collective pile of human stilts. Paula stood in the center of the jumble of humanity, curtailing the emotional outbursts grinding inside her. She remained head down watching the wetness swirl around her soaked heels and splattering her entire body. Her new bloody and devilish form still avoided making the slightest eye contact with the murderous character before her.

"Finish it up," Sebastian barked, seemingly over the initial grand slaughter already. Jinx nodded the saturated, wrinkly mask toward Sebastian and went for their heads next.

Those that were still coherent put their hands up (and inadvertently the hands of their neighbor due to the handcuffs) to no avail. It only led to more violent mathematics. The division was inescapable, but the number they chose was up to them. Many had lost the fight when they lost their legs. They just let the saw make its way straight to their throat or face in hopes of attaining the quickest ending.

The majority of their skulls were not completely detached. Many dangled chunks or were just void of the essential life-filling that any non-desensitized mortal would feel nauseated in seeing absent. What was moments ago a circle of life was now a ring of death. The torn-up tissue that surrounded Paula pumped out its insides and twitched, still mostly bonded together. As the slaughter crawled closer toward her, she wished she could somehow crawl inside herself.

Jinx set the saw down on the floor, miming energy depletion with a Charlie Chaplin-esque charm. The jester's buffoonery couldn't have been less comical; there were no lengths that could garner a smile with the tier of anarchy that surrounded them. There was no way to pull a chuckle out from the hell that Jinx and Sebastian had manufactured.

"Now, this is starting to look like a goddamn massacre if you ask me! But I think we still have one more to go..." Sebastian said, turning his head back toward Jasmine.

The waitress had backed herself into the corner beside the stage. A restrictive paralysis had come over her as she watched him walk over to Jinx and take hold of the DNA-drenched slaughter device.

"You let them down," Sebastian said, pointing back to the heaping disaster comprised of her fellow carved-up associates.

Jasmine started to lose control of her bowels, her black pants moistened, and a warm yellow puddle formed as Sebastian started to close in on her.

"Darling, are you really fucking pissing all over yourself? If you're pissing all over the floor at my wedding, then you're pissing all over me! You filthy swine, you disgusting trough troll!"

He lunged toward her with the saw spinning but something inside her switched; somehow, she'd regained her motor abilities. But for every fortunate happening, there are ten misfortunes — the balance was unavoidable on that day or the following.

As Jasmine side-stepped the buzzing metal, her curly ponytail was not able to evade getting snarled in the revolutions. It was only a moment before the rotations caused the back of her scalp to be pulled into the nefarious device. It sliced into her, deeply shredding the bone and causing her brain matter to fling about and pepper Sebastian's perfectly-pressed tux.

He pressed it deep into her, watched her eyes begin to roll around before her flailing arms found rest. He removed his finger from the trigger and Jasmine dropped down onto her hands and knees. The ruined girl looked like a stillborn fetus wiggling about directionless. Sebastian walked back over to the buttery slick of dehydrated urine that she'd left behind and pointed downward.

"You know, in Indonesia, the bride and groom are both expected to go three days without using the bathroom? Sounds a bit extreme, but in that culture, it's supposed to symbolize the strengthening of the newlywed's bond. And look at you, you can't even go a few hours. Your relief is incredibly selfish…"

Jasmine remained shaking without control on the ground, still overwhelmed by the vile acts inflicted upon her.

"You hear me, you cunt? You see the fucking mess you made at my wedding!? Well, now you're gonna clean it up, come and clean it up NOW and maybe, just maybe I won't cut you again."

Somehow, Jasmine was still computing what he was saying despite her severe head trauma. In a more than miraculous display of effort, she clawed her way sluggishly over to the puddle of piss. The onlookers grimaced as she dragged herself forward pathetically. As she inched forward with each claw-like motion, some of her fingernails began to snap off and start bleeding in the process.

"Faster, go faster, cunt!" he commanded until she had finally pulled herself back into her warm secretion.

She slid the arm of her shirt into the puddle while blood rained down, mixing into the yellow pool. She looked like a malfunctioning maid stuck in fetish mode. Her incredible determination was valiant but nothing could be enough to satisfy Sebastian.

"No! Put it back where it came from! I can't have you walking around my wedding guests smelling like a damn hooker, can I?! I know my wife wouldn't approve of that..." Sebastian looked up at Taylor as he instructed Jasmine while kicking her arm away viciously.

"Slurp it up, c'mon, bitch, you look like you've been around the block a few times. I'm sure this ain't the first golden shower you've been involved with." He winked at the mass of horrified onlookers while she continued to bleed and began sucking up the now orangey liquid.

She was able to ingest a surprising quantity. It was more than Sebastian would have believed to have been possible in her state. For the first time that evening, Sebastian was legitimately impressed. While what Cindy displayed during the cannibalism contest was quite unexpected, she hadn't had a saw scramble her brains just before the whistle.

"That's a good girl. A very, VERY good girl. Alright, you've shown that you can follow my directions and, as promised, I won't cut you again."

Sebastian raised his foot up and drove his heel into the area of split skull in the back of her head. Her teeth shattered, crushing against the slick floor and her brains erupted upward like wet carnal fireworks. The ever-present muddled gasps of those stomaching the humiliating and horrifying spectacle peaked.

The slurping stopped. The squirming stopped. Any semblance of movement stopped, as a definite stillness took hold of her. Those watching felt disgust, terror, hate, but most tellingly, envy. She had what they all wanted.

Jasmine was able to "get it over with." Jasmine was dead. As for the rest of them, they would have to wait their turn.

HUMILIATION

Sebastian had been standing by the stage silently for almost fifteen minutes. Jinx sat by idly; creepy jester eyes submerged in the depths of the strange mask and fixed on the cowering, uneasy crowd. Maybe they were uneasy because Jinx continued to straddle the detonator so menacingly.

The idea that the entire room exploding hinged on the actions of the discernibly disturbed figure had left a constant panic festering inside everyone. To that point, there hadn't been a dull moment throughout the entire reception.

Taylor's eyes scanned over the jester and made their way to the crowd. She'd been sizing up the creep's body, trying to get an idea, any idea to sprout in her head. While riding the constant carousel of terror, it was hard to think but she was doing her best to fight her way through it.

Who was Sebastian's mysterious silent helping hand? She didn't have the slightest inclination that Sebastian was a psychopath for the entire duration of their relationship. Never a flare-up in his temper, questionable interests, or anything worthy of raising a flag over. She didn't even know he had friends outside of work.

Then again, she didn't particularly spend a lot of time with him or pay him any mind. How could she expect to know? Everything she saw was contrary to what she was seeing presently. In her pain-saturated eyes, Sebastian was just a softie who had erratically tapped into a whole different stratosphere. One that required meticulous plotting, a lack of emotion, and the gastric capacity for evil the likes of which she'd never imagined.

One thing that was running through her mind was how exactly two sick people came to find each other. To her, it seemed logical to think that if someone were to speak about committing carnage of the nature she was entrenched in, that odds were, the person on the other side of the conversation would run away and report them.

But upon further inspection of that thought, she realized history was riddled with countless pairs of deranged individuals that sought the same type of sinister solace that was only found within their twisted companionship.

Maybe the odds were better than she thought. Maybe the disturbed delinquents were breeding at a record rate. It didn't matter anyway, there would be no solution in crunching the numbers. They had found each other and the threat was real.

Taylor knew tons of people, but realistically, how many of them would truly want to hurt her and potentially exterminate her entire web of friends and family? Forty, maybe fifty percent?

As she continued to assess the path that led her head-first into the grim event, the self-reflection was cutting. She'd never really taken time to think about the people she stepped on en route to the top of the mountain. But the more she pondered the puzzle, the more it was becoming blatantly clear that there were A LOT of people who hated her.

How many people had she wronged? How many men had she manipulated? How many relationships had she wrecked? How many hearts had she stolen? How many guys had she fucked? How many girls had she fucked? The immersive questions continued to parade through her mind, and while all of them were valid, a better question was whose sanity had she stretched?

Whoever this individual was, they were equally as cold and heartless as Sebastian. What if they weren't even tied to her? That was also a possibility, maybe Sebastian had done some manipulating of his own. Maybe while the cat was away, the mouse had played and found another sick puppy.

Sebastian had been hiding so much shit that it would no longer be surprising if she didn't know the jester at all. That wasn't her gut intuition, but it certainly would've explained why Sebastian wasn't phased in the slightest when she'd return home in the late night or early morning with evidence of infidelity shamelessly plastered upon her.

It was simple: he'd been knee-deep in his own debauchery. The only difference was, his decadence was a lot more dangerous than contracting a potential STD (however, it was just as well hidden). But a few doses of penicillin weren't going to cure this clusterfuck, that was for sure.

Speaking of clusterfuck, her eyes had made their way over to the table of her former (and current) pound pals that she'd so boldly decided to extend an invitation to. The amount of muscle sitting at the table was jaw-dropping. These boys had better racks than half the broads in the joint. She was sure they'd started regretting their decisions already.

The regret had begun to swell inside her. The wise ass, blatantly disrespectful move of not just inviting a former fling to a wedding, but arranging an entire table of these dickheads to share stories seemed like a fruitless and potentially fatal rib now.

If Sebastian had the wherewithal to arrange an up until that point flawless mass execution, then he most certainly knew a lot more than he was letting on. He knew about them, he had to.

She felt thankful that they had done little to attract any attention to themselves thus far but it was inevitable. As the numbers dwindled, it would eventually become a topic for Sebastian's bizarre spoken word. He was hell-bent on interacting with everyone by the night's end. It was definitely just a matter of time before the dirty laundry was aired out in front of what was left of the crowd.

Taylor started to notice some uneasy whispers amongst the testosterone-rampant foursome. They were the type of men who were used to being in control at all times. If something was not to their liking, they had the bravado to fix it. But today was a tad different. Their swagger had been circumcised and all they could do was wait.

"What if we all just rush 'em?" Rocky floated the idea again.

"Keep your fucking voice down. You animal!" Kwan whispered sternly.

Brick looked up to Rocky with fear in his eyes, "I'm in," he conceded.

"Are you guys as dumb as you look? The clown has a fucking military-grade machine gun and a button that turns us to dust with one touch. No. The only thing we can do is hope he lets us live. If we do what he says, it's a possibility still," Luke explained, trying to reason with them. But the expressions the group projected seemed divided.

"Maybe you're good with drinking your own piss and getting run through like forest lumber, but I ain't going out like a bitch, okay? He's just been sitting there doing nothing this whole time, it's now or never," Rocky argued.

"Luke is right, if you get up, you're dead. There isn't much else to it. Waiting is the only way, or maybe if one of them comes close enough, we could make a move. He said he was leaving survivors, didn't he?" Kwan wanted to stay as low profile as possible, but keeping these meatheads in line was no task for a novice.

"SURVIVOR. That's singular, fuck-stick! That means potentially only one of us lives but probably none because look at how many other stupid people are around here."

Rocky's correction was warranted but Luke recalled the exact verbiage. "At least one person to tell the story. 'At least one' were his exact words. Technically, there could be more than one."

"Have you looked at the dancefloor lately? If you can look out there and think that this fuckin' whack-job is leaving more than one, then it's *you* that needs your fuckin' head examined."

Rocky finished his whispers just as Sebastian made his way back to his feet. He closed his eyes, inhaling deeply, and then paused for a moment before letting the air out. He was taking it all in like he'd just sniffed a fine wine and it was now swirling around on his pallet. His eyelids fluttered before finding consistency. He looked out at his audience, readying himself to start speaking again.

"This is what I was attempting to explain to you earlier. If we're just killing out of convenience and squeezing in as much violence as we can because the fear that it will be over any moment is always hovering over us, well, that's quite a waste, isn't it?"

Sebastian slowly poured out a quarter glass of vodka from a bottle he'd snatched away from behind the bar earlier. He slung back the clear alcohol and looked toward his guests.

"You need time to understand it, digest it. Let it air out for a moment and take it in before what comes next. You know, I don't believe heaven is a place, I believe it's a state of mind. And it's different for everyone," he explained, walking closer to the steroid stable of beefcake.

"For some, it's dancing or a good steak, for others, it's the more traditional understanding we were raised to look forward to. For someone like me, it probably looks a lot closer to something out of Dante's Inferno. The variance is important, it allows flexibility, it allows boundless options. For example, you, sir, I don't believe we've formally met before.

Brick, is your preferred forename, is that correct?"

"Um, yeah," he nodded, discomfort arising from the fact that he already knew who he was.

"Imagine that? Named after a building material, how original." Sebastian looked toward Taylor who now stood beside the blood-covered table that had traumatized Paula and Cindy.

"Honey, is this the one that left his liquid babies caked into your extensions that beautiful evening when I proposed to you?"

The crowd let out a gasp. It was good to know that Jerry Springer-style drama still had a place, even when it was surrounded by absolute depravity.

Taylor was unequivocally flabbergasted; she didn't know how to respond. *How could he tell I have extensions?* she thought as her face rushed full of rosy blush. *Also, he let the cat out of the bag about the whole hook-up situation… Sebastian knows much more than he's letting on…* she continued on with the poorly prioritized thoughts in her simple mind.

"It's okay, I'm not mad, baby. I mean, clearly you thought you were playing me, but now you know what the deal is. So, just answer the goddamn question before you really do tick me off."

"No, it was Rocky," she responded with disgrace slathering her tone.

The crowd didn't seem stunned, it could've been that they were all already just as aware of Taylor's infidelities as Sebastian was, or maybe the fact that publicly revealing a cheater was peanuts compared to the breed of mayhem they'd all just been smacked in the face with.

A hot redness started swelling to the surface of

Rocky's block-like head. He could feel the multitude of eyeballs targeting him. Even he was smart enough to realize he was in deep shit.

"Okay, okay, you're right. I must have gotten it mixed up. Brick here is the one that boned you last night, do I have it straight now?"

It took Taylor a few seconds, but this time she nodded her head slowly in defeat.

"Say it," Sebastian demanded.

"Yes. You're right."

"In fact, Kwan and Luke have both been inside you recently too, haven't they?"

"Yes."

"Well… it appears you certainly have a type."

Sebastian circled the table, placing his fingertips on the shoulder of each of the behemoths. He didn't seem angry, more amused than anything. As he made his way around, he selected a word to describe each man that he recited for the group.

"Bulging… shredded… shallow… and… stupid. I think it's also interesting to note that while I'm directing a different word toward each of you, all of these descriptors are interchangeable. You're all the same. You all exhibit a pitiful plethora of identical traits and tendencies."

Sebastian suddenly jerked his focus away from the bodybuilders and back toward Taylor.

"This is so predictable. You're so predictable it's pathetic. It didn't take much research for me to comprehend that mental capacity isn't something you seem to see value in. No, you've always been obsessed with the shell. The gym memberships, the muscle shirts, the spray tans. Inside, they could be as hollow as a chocolate bunny and it wouldn't phase you one bit."

"Chocolate bunny! I want a chocolate bunny!" Christopher yelped through the cracks of his father's fingers. Anthony tried to hush him but it was too late; Sebastian had keyed in on the boy again. A bizarre correlation began stirring about in his mind.

"No, Dad, it's okay. You don't have to hold him back. In fact, I'm glad he decided to speak up. Ironically, it makes sense. It all makes perfect sense, now. Your brother is retarded…" he said, sticking the left thumb out as if calculating his theory.

"And you've invited an entire table of retards — which, might I add, you've been fucking with consistency — to our wedding."

He let his index finger join his thumb and looked up at her, "So, there must be some kind of pent-up sexual tension between you and Christopher, right?"

A stunned silence resonated all around.

"N-No!" Taylor stammered out.

"What did you say to me?"

"You told me to tell the truth about everything. I'm telling you the truth, Sebastian, I swear to you." The waterworks started up, causing her make-up to run over the retreads of sadness again.

Anthony had reached a boiling point inside, the scalding indignation he felt was edging to where it was nearly uncontrollable. He couldn't let him keep talking to his little girl the way he was, but at that moment, he still had no say in the matter.

He thought about trying to take him out but caught a glimpse of the maniacal jester mere yards away. Jinx's heathenish eyes hovered coldly, hiding like a coward behind the mask. There was nothing relaxed about the intensity the clown was gripping the AK with. The sicko didn't take a second off, at any moment, the barrel was ready to be fired. The odds of making a move that would alter the power pyramid were shit and they never seemed ready to shift.

"Come over here, now, Taylor," Sebastian commanded, curling his fingers in towards his chest. Taylor reluctantly shuffled to the table where her family was seated, and like a dog to her master, she waited for further direction.

"I want you to repeat after me," he paused for a moment, returning back to the thought he'd already moved on from, "and I don't want you to say it because your life hangs in the balance, or because you're afraid. I want you to say it because it's the fucking truth, do you understand me?"

"Yes," she replied, sniffling the snot up that was running from her nose.

"Let me see it, I want to hold it right now because I'm not convinced I won't need it momentarily." Sebastian reached outward toward Jinx, beckoning for the AK. Jinx handed it over without making a comment and watched Sebastian grip it tightly, like he was doing everything possible to control himself. He wasn't aiming it at anyone but he was more than ready to as his eyes again locked onto his wife.

"All I do is fuck retards…" Sebastian said, watching her closely.

"All I do is fuck retards…" she recited.

"And that's why…"

"And that's why…"

"I'm going to fuck my retard brother."

The chorus of huffs and gulps from the crowd

was becoming redundant. Anthony's eyes began to glaze over while his molars ground against each other. Taylor tried to finish speaking but the words just weren't coming out.

"Well?" Sebastian asked, watching her squirm while her mind raced thinking up a response.

"I-I can't. I just can't," Taylor replied, frightened to the core.

"Why the fuck not?"

"Because it's wrong! It's evil, Sebastian!" she yelped, beginning to lose control.

"Is it because your dad is here? Is he making it weird?" he inquired as he started to elevate his barrel. Anthony slowly removed his hands from Christopher and pushed him away.

"No, please!" Taylor yelled.

Anthony didn't have time to get his boy out of harm's way and pull his gun. Taylor's begging was instantly overshadowed by the disturbing pops of the automatic spraying. A half-dozen or so apricot-sized holes blew into Anthony's toned chest before the force tipped his chair backwards and he spilled over onto the floor.

Anthony thrashed about restlessly, choking on his own blood while the contents of his torso spilled out of the gaping hole in his lower back. Taylor fell to the ground beside her father and could see that his condition was critical. His lips fluttered rapidly as he emitted a series of dire coughs. He wouldn't be coming back from the shots he took.

She could plainly see that one of his lungs was punctured and dangling halfway out of his back. She reached around him and tried to hold the deflated organ up and prevent it from falling as best she could. The feeling of his warm, quaking insides was a sickening and inexplicable sensation.

Taylor held his head up and immediately noticed something swirling in her father's pupils that was highly abnormal. It was something that Taylor had never seen him project, at least as far as she'd ever known. It was uncertainty.

His wife, Lisa, who up until that point had been suffocating all emotion, began to unravel. She stood up and charged Sebastian, cursing him carelessly, any sane thought had finally evaporated. Something upstairs had snapped and left her with a total disregard for her own safety.

It wasn't hard for him to counter her action; he simply sidestepped and swung the butt of the rifle into her cheek. A lengthy gash formed, stretching all the way up to her earlobe. A couple of molars in the rear of her mouth were loosened as she fell to the ground unconscious.

"C'mon, we're family now, we can't be fighting like this! Especially in front of guests!" Sebastian remarked sarcastically.

Taylor watched her father start to fade. He was gargling a hot broth of reddish gore and choked, accidentally spitting the wad all over Taylor's face. She was quite accustomed to having a mass of warm fluid coating her grill but never this hue.

In his dying moments, Anthony's mangled left hand lifted his blazer up discreetly, showing his daughter the gleaming steel of the revolver that was tucked away into the hidden holster inside. As she wiped the blood from her eyes, they widened.

She caught a glimpse of the weapon but before she could react or think about going for it, another handful of shells deconstructed Anthony's face. What remained of his head fell backwards, he was now merely a mindless puzzle of deformity and death.

Sebastian's heartless tone invaded her ears again, "Get up now, bitch. If you wanna give Mommy a better chance than ol' Pop, you would heed my warnings."

Sebastian was growing more and more ruthless by the second. Any trace of the man she knew prior had vanished or maybe it was just never there in the first place. It seemed that the madman was in control of everyone but himself.

She felt like she didn't have a choice, her dad had ceased any movement. His final act was one that he hoped might give his family a chance at survival, even though he would have no shot at exhaling beside them when it was finally over. However, the fact remained that if she went for the gun, she would be dead long before she got a chance to use it.

Thankfully, she knew how to handle a firearm. Anthony had taken her to shatter a few bottles years ago with what looked to be the same piece. She caught on quickly and enjoyed their homemade shooting range. Anthony had figured based on his little girl's personality and everlasting enemies list that she could do with learning how to protect herself. However, even he was surprised that Taylor was interested. Even though she was a princess girly girl, she was a damn good shot.

Taylor understood that she couldn't use the gun at the moment, but at least she knew it was there. She could only cross her fingers that an opportunity would somehow present itself if she lasted long enough. Still, part of her considered the discovery a bad omen since her father was in the process of expiring most likely with similar thoughts in his own head that had failed to manifest.

"Come over here now and get on your knees beside your dreamboat bro," Sebastian instructed, pointing to the floor with the gun barrel.

"Papa, where'd you get all that jelly from? STOP! NO, PLEASE STOP ALL THAT JELLY, PAPA!" Christopher took a gander downward at his leaky hero and was still understandably not grasping the finality of the scene before him.

"Whoa, calm down a moment, fella. You know Papa's a real rascal sometimes, he's just resting up… Let's just let him relax for a bit, but in the meantime, you wanna open a gift?"

The boy's eyes lit up as Taylor's filled with more water. Sebastian looked back at Jinx with a devious smirk, "Well, we don't wanna keep him waiting, grab a little something for the kid. Grab the *special* one."

Jinx walked over and retrieved a small square box enveloped in neon pink wrapping paper and returned to Christopher, setting it down in front of him. The playful boy slapped it a few times and shook it around before tossing it back on the table like a lion rejecting its cub.

"Well, go ahead, have at it, kid. I got this one special, just for you," Sebastian explained.

Christopher seemed unamused, but to Taylor's relief, did as he was instructed. He peeled back the cheap wrapper and ripped into the thin cardboard shell. The contents revealed were four individual pairs of handcuffs, a roll of duct tape, and a mask that was extremely peculiar in appearance.

The stretchy black material was clearly some kind of strange custom design that sought to block out particular senses of whoever donned it. There was no way to see or smell through the leathery hide as it was crafted to encompass the entire head.

Additionally, there were steel plates bonded onto sound-neutralizing earplugs that were fixed to each side of the mask. The only senses that the skull leech didn't render useless were touch and taste. The single mouth hole was all that gave access to oxygen but there was a catch. The entire boundary of the air opening was encircled by a shiny razor-sharp metal that served as the lips.

"Okay, kid, I lied a little bit. This gift isn't *entirely* for you. The cuffs are yours though. Glad we bought these in bulk." Sebastian smiled as Jinx took the wrist-locks away from him.

"But the mask here is actually for your big sister," Sebastian continued.

Jinx proceeded to grab the confused boy by each of his limbs and fasten the chrome restrictors to different parts of the chair, crippling Christopher's movement entirely. Next, Jinx grabbed hold of the sinister mask and tossed it into the blood-puddled floor in front of Taylor.

"This is a real fun game!" Christopher chimed in.

"Darn right it is! Wait until you see just how fun it gets! Are you excited?" Sebastian asked.

"I'm excited! I'm excited!" Christopher shrieked.

"Wonderful! Put the fucking mask on, bitch," Sebastian commanded Taylor in a stern tone.

"PLEASE! Don't make me... don't make me do this!" Taylor cried.

Sebastian glanced over toward Jinx, "I think she's gonna need some help."

While Sebastian's AK remained fixed on his lady, the perverse helper scooped up the mask and began to muscle it over the terrified bride's cranium. It was an awkward task, like trying to put a condom on a cousin.

Taylor gagged as the still warm and fresh blood that was her father's coated the saturated rawhide and somehow found its way into her mouth. As the guise blocked out some of her senses, those that still remained were heightened. The taste of thick life-force was nauseating. She spat out her father's fluid in an attempt to avoid vomiting, but she did so carelessly and neglected the razor portal that was fixed at her mouth's end.

As her slick tongue flicked the rosy saliva off her palate, the tip of the muscle made contact with the shining steel demonstrating just how dangerous it was. About a half-inch-worth of her tongue was spliced off and fell into a freshly created pool on her lower jaw.

Screams emanated as she grabbed at her face (even though she couldn't get to it) and skinned her ring finger. Crimson leaked all over the massive love diamond that Sebastian had given her as she contemplated if she should spit the severed chunk of tongue out of her mouth.

Her warped husband laughed, seeing the humor and irony behind her unknowingly mutilating, of all fingers, that particular finger. Moments later, she ejected the wad of humanity as her lungs pumped furiously and her back contracted.

"My fucking tongue!" she cried with a new lisp

now in play that detracted heavily from her normally cocky demeanor.

"I'm fuckin' deformed, you sick bastard!" It came out as 'thick bathtard,' almost making her sound intellectually on par with her brother. "It won't stop bleeding! My mouth keeps filling up!" she shrieked.

Jinx pulled up the steel plate embedded into the mask over her left ear and allowed her to listen.

Sebastian watched a massive cascade of crimson drop down onto the hardwood as he answered her.

"Well, you better get to work then," he replied, snatching up the duct tape off the table. "Once you pop the retard's oral cherry, we can get that bleeding stopped for you."

Sebastian started to spiral the gray tape roll all around the fantastically obedient Christopher's lips and neck before slowly working his way up to the eyes and forehead. In a matter of seconds, he was a mummified gray giggling blank slate.

"Now, remember, you can't stop until he cums in your mouth, that's the rules."

"I won't fucking do it, go to hell, Sebastian!"

"I think it's a lot more likely that you'll be going before me, honey, but who am I to judge…" Sebastian explained, handing the machine gun over to Jinx.

He extracted an expandable blade from inside his pant and cut out a large square patch of cloth above Christopher's cock. The excitable boy squirmed about, breathing heavily through his mouth; it was hard to tell if he was enjoying the game anymore.

"Look at the sheer size of this fuckin' thing!" Sebastian squawked. He grabbed a firm hold of the beastly, vein-riddled pipe, "Jesus, you got a permit for this thing, kid?"

Sebastian knelt down beside Taylor and put his lips to her exposed ear and the knife to her throat, "Either you get going now and give him a chance to live, or I can cut his prick off, put it in a blender, and feed it to you that way."

Taylor's tears evoked no pity, he plunged the tip of the steel into her sternum and drove it back and forth, creating a small cavity of gore. Her pleas didn't deter him from pulling out the knife tip and creating long oozing slashes over her pretty shoulders next. Sebastian's violence was always prompt and savage, the sadist in him forever aroused by her cries for mercy. His harsh malice and negligence seemed to have finally inspired an attitude adjustment.

"Please, I'm sorry! Stop cutting me! Stop cutting me!" she begged, now feeling the throbbing pain fostered by the many lacerations.

Sebastian quickly collapsed the knife and put it back into his pocket. He stared out to the crowd of horrified onlookers, no doubt imagining what choice they might have made.

"It's very simple, people, it can be easy or it can be hard. But rest assured, when I tell you to do something, one way or another, you're damn-well gonna do it."

"Don't move," he ordered Taylor as he pressed one hand under a gash in her torso and used the other to squeeze blood out of it. She banged her feet into the floor, trying to bite her tongue as pain surged from the manual liquid purge.

Once he had collected a significant sum of blood, he walked back over to Christopher who was still

113

fidgeting about in an uncomfortable manner while his fat horse-like cock flapped about. Sebastian dispensed his sister's secretions all over the massive tool, leaving it wet and red. Then he knelt down on one knee beside the boy and started stroking the goliath shaft.

"You better hope that he's a shower, not a grower. Either way, I think if you're careful enough, you can suck him off without skinning his entire shaft. The hole in your mask looks to be just big enough... but you're really gonna need to concentrate here, he's got a fuckin' monster attached to him so there's not a hell of a lotta room for error. The quicker you get his rocks off, the better the end result."

Sebastian locked onto the area where Taylor should have been as a perverse grin overtook him. "He's nice and ready for you now, hard as heaven. It's time to come and get it, honey," Sebastian snickered.

He continued to jerk the throbbing meat and call out to his wife, "Come here, baby, come and get him..." he whispered, watching her crawl blindly through the half coagulated stretches of her father's hemoglobin.

Once she got in range, he guided her gently by the back of her head into Christopher's now erect penis. He was vigilant and wanted to ensure she got a fair shake at the task.

"That's a girl. Here, grab it yourself now," he huffed, placing her hand at the base of his dick.

He pushed her head slightly forward and then a bit to the right like a barber searching for the proper angle during a haircut.

"Okay, your mouth is right over his cock... NOW! If you go directly down on him and hold him firm, you're set up for success," he proclaimed before closing up the metal plating over her earhole.

Blood rained down from Taylor's leaking mouth all over Christopher's already cherry cock. She opened her lips, creating a firm edge. She tasted her salty tears pulled down by her mask, stinging the open wounds of her oral cavity. Fear bubbled inside; she didn't want to hurt her brother but she couldn't shake the thought of how disgusting what she was about to do was.

Even more concerning than the repulsive aspect of the act was the clear and present danger. Based on her own encounter with the exterior of the mask, she knew that one wrong slant or slip and she might sever his penis or peel it with the ease of a banana.

Her neck was stiff as she descended on him carefully. Her heart thrashed about, pulsating her grisly sternum as the perspiration accumulated with each inch that was disappearing between them. Gradually, she tasted him enter her wet mouth and he tasted like neglect. Through the blood, sweat, and tears, Christopher's elongated and unwashed jaw-breaker was salty and pungent like it'd just been pulled out of a street scrounger's ripened asshole.

Her rancid disrelish had caught her off guard; she expected him to be cleaner. She gagged, fighting the urge to vomit, it would cause movement and things might go south fast. She decided that deepthroating him would be the best solution to keep his dirty dick safe. The enormous uncircumcised bulge bullied her uvula backward and filled up her tiny throat as she continued onward like a carny sword swallower.

The amount of wiggle room in her esophagus was dangerously slim. She continued to gag but remained still. She tried to breathe through her nose but the mask was so tight, it restricted the airflow.

While Taylor struggled to efficiently trigger her brother's ejaculation (with some admittedly bomb head), Sebastian watched. He glanced back over to the table of her former fuck buddies and looked at Brick. He sat terrified by the highly disturbing presentation.

"I bet you're gonna miss that, huh? I know I sure as hell will."

Brick stayed silent as his testosterone-troubled frame shook and he sobbed like a little girl. The other meatheads attempted to console each other, fearing that their own fates could be much worse than the horror that progressed and contorted before them. The wave of emotion was probably derived from the thought that the evil spectacle was merely a sick form of eerie foreshadowing.

"What the fuck!" Lisa yelled through her recent facial alterations.

She'd somewhat regained consciousness and stumbled upon the offensive incestual event which Sebastian had orchestrated. The sickening feeling crushed her guts and mind — it distracted her so effectively that she didn't even notice her freshly modified tooth gaps and split lips.

The confusion and horror screamed from her surface. Sebastian shifted his gaze from the arranged love affair back to his mother-in-law. "She shouldn't have to watch this. No mother should be put through this… it's too much. So we can ensure she doesn't, Jinx, please break her orbital bones and mash her fucking eyeballs to a pulp."

As Jinx set off toward the mortified mother, Sebastian headed back to the stage. He extracted a lengthy machete from the sliding panel underneath the stairs and promptly reapproached the twisted sex act. He set his feet behind Christopher and looked down at Taylor frozen in place, still oblivious with her senses snuffed out and carefully deepthroating her brother.

"If he's getting head, then so am I..." Sebastian announced.

Sebastian raised the machete and sawed into Christopher's spine while his frame began to shake and gyrate uncontrollably. As he pulled off the boy's tape-layered head, two eruptions commenced in graphic unison. There was the release from the foursome of jugular veins that had been opened at the throat and the second from his first load of steaming hot sperm that rocketed down his big sister's windpipe.

His first orgasm was a fucking doozy, like milking a cow that had months of buildup. As the creamy barrage of shots pelted her flesh tunnel, she felt a microscopic measure of liberation. Taylor's body shook about just as violently as her brother's. The raunchy blend of vomit and cum slimed its way forcefully out of both her nostrils and trickled down her lips.

Taylor stood up and lost her balance and fell tumbling backwards. The mask metal dug into his rod, skinning from the base of his shaft up to the tip of his dick. It came off cleaner than peeling a potato. The strip of pared penis flesh dangled over the top. It only remained attached due to the uncircumcised casing held in place by the crusty strength of a cheesy ring of foul smegma. The barf-worthy bondage was an adhesive for the ages.

She tore the leather like an animal before finally ripping the mask from her head. Upon finding her facial freedom again, she regurgitated a foul cyclone of undigested food, blood, and cum. It rained out of her pie hole and onto Christopher's motor boating red bone. Boogers and bile splashed from both nostrils as she caught the first glimpse of her brother; his memory to be forever tarnished by the final acts of skeeve inflicted upon him.

She loosened her grip and the scarring mask fell, landing in the messy waste pile on the floor beside her. Taylor looked for Christopher's head but it was nowhere in front of her; it was gone. She followed the liquid exploding from his throat down to her own personal handy work. The chaos ingrained upon him was incomprehensible, it was a stamp on his downtrodden existence; the end of days.

A feminine screech drew her attention from her annihilated brother's convulsing corpse. Sebastian stood beside Jinx holding a sword-like device and what she could only assume was Christopher's decapitated top. Jinx was keeping busy driving the butt of the gun into Lisa's head.

Taylor watched, speechless, as her defenseless mother's cheekbones collapsed in on themselves and her nose turned sideways. The jester kept going until the buttstock was covered with steaming hunks of her skin and face. The sick bastard continued further until her face became one with the wall she was slumped against. Jinx didn't stop until it looked like a wig was sitting on top of an unmade pile of pig slop.

Sebastian turned back to her as Jinx let off a full clip of shells that tore through her guts. "Your mom, she got real upset when she saw what you were up to, being the fucking perverted slut that you are. So, we made it so you can't upset her anymore…"

Taylor stood in a state of quiet devastation — it was as if she'd just been struck by a missile. Her entire immediate family had been put down hard in a cruel and extraordinary manner. She was finally able to stop throwing up, having emptied all of her stomach's contents, despite a lingering feeling of internal illness. The detachment of her tongue-tip left blood still pouring without fail from her jaws.

"That's right, babe, I almost forgot, we gotta patch you up. We can't have you bleeding out, no, we're just getting started here."

He wandered back to the same area of the stage as before. This time, he retrieved a bulky navy-blue cylindrical canister. He unscrewed a knob and used a sparker clipped to the side of the device to create the flame. A working blowtorch was a horrifying blend of both good and bad news for Taylor.

"Hold her down on the table," Sebastian said.

The jester's compliance was unquestionable and, within seconds, Jinx had swept Taylor off her feet and had her laid out on the table. She just let it happen, like a rape victim that the fight had already escaped from.

Sebastian produced a pair of pliers from his pants and quickly pounced on her. While Jinx had a vice-like clutch on both the top and bottom of her head, Sebastian used the steel grips to clamp down on the center of her oozing tongue.

Taylor writhed in anguish as the flame started to sear the gash. A bottomless black crust appeared, cauterizing the once drippy opening. Sebastian looked into the havoc festering inside her pupils and whispered, "I always wanted to melt in your mouth."

THE PEANUT
GALLERY

Jinx sat frozen on the steps of the stage, ominously overseeing the crowd while Sebastian laid a few yards behind him with a balled-up tablecloth under his head, napping. They could hear his slight snore leaking through the PA system via the mini-mic clipped to his collar. The crazed groom was truly savoring every single moment of it, planned intermissions included.

Taylor sat a short distance away at the table closest to the stage beside her headless brother who no longer remained handcuffed to his chair. They'd piled his annihilated corpse in front of her and left the ruined bodies of her parents beside him to comprise the remainder of the gory pile.

She could have never imagined her special day would be *this* special. The magical evening would be quite memorable, but for all the wrong reasons…

That fucking bastard. I should have never even given him the time of day! I gave him the best days — no, MONTHS — of my life! I wish I had known it was gonna be over sooner… I would've taken more pictures, made more posts, worked a little harder for those likes. I didn't leave enough to make a real impression, I'm just another pretty face. They'll never remember me for the good things now! I'll always be that girl that got murdered on her wedding day with a bunch of fucking nobodies… Taylor thought to herself somberly.

Suddenly, it dawned on her. Taylor's heart started to race with a newfound hope. *Maybe they'll make a 20/20 or Dateline about me?!*

After the conveyer belt of vanity produced almost any self-centered ponderance imaginable, she began to think more rationally; *the gun! I want to fucking kill him so bad! But Dad's right in front of me… No, it would be too obvious if I just started searching him in front of everyone. Actually, there are way too many people still alive anyway. I'm gonna need to wait for the numbers to dwindle a little bit more before I make my move. I'm the bride, he's gotta keep me around a little while longer at least. There's no way he's gonna kill me before the rest of the nobodies. Surely, he would have done it already. I just have to keep waiting for the right opportunity…*

***

In the distance, what remained of Sebastian's family looked on. Hana hadn't said a word since she'd seen her son send a barrage of bullets into her husband, leaving him crumpled against the elegant wall of the Biltmore. She simply sat still as a mannequin with her wide eyes but in a state of shutdown.

Uncle Ivan attempted to keep the ladies calm as best he could. His wife, Olga, and daughter, Nina, had been justifiably hysterical for some time. He was grateful they hadn't made a scene because, aside from the faint oddly romantic background music that DJ Buttaz had been forced to play, you could hear a pin drop.

He draped his jacket over his brother's destroyed expression in an attempt to remove some of the crippling horror they were all surrounded by. Thankfully, Olga and Nina's seats were facing the wall so they didn't have to look at the dancefloor that looked more like the murder room inside of a slaughterhouse.

"What have you done, Sebastian?" Uncle Ivan whispered to himself.

"We are all going to die!" Olga wept.

Nina's sniffle started to accelerate. Her heavy breathing left her body inflating and deflating like a blow-up pool float.

"Shhhh!" Ivan put his finger up to his lips. "You must stay calm."

"Save us, Ivan, you must do something!"

"What? What must I do? The boy is lost, I don't know how to fix him."

"I will not sit around and wait for death!"

"Olga, calm yourself, please. For Nina."

She had almost entirely forgotten about her petrified daughter sitting beside her. The survival instincts had blinded her, all Olga could think about was saving her own hide from the pulverizing end that she'd seen so many others come to find.

Olga looked into Nina's tear-squirting eyes and rubbed her back gently. Then shifted her gaze back to her husband.

"What will we do?" she begged the question.

"I know you are scared, I am as well. There is no escape, he has seen to that. Only option is reason with him, or overthrow him. But I don't see how this is possible…"

Uncle Ivan was being as realistic as he could. He'd gone through the scenarios in his head over and over. There was no easy out. As he watched his sick nephew go on for hours, tearing friends and family limb from limb, he couldn't help but feel an overall feeling of impending doom crushing him.

"I know you don't like answer, but we must wait. If I get chance to stop him, I will," Ivan promised.

"Daddy, I don't want to be hurt like those other people," Nina wailed.

"I know, baby, I know. I love you, sweet pea, and know that Papa will protect you," Ivan replied in a shaken tone that couldn't sound less empty of confidence.

"That's right, you have nothing to worry about," Olga mumbled on the verge of tears, trying to reaffirm for the poor girl.

Ivan turned to the side and back to Hana who was still as stoic as ever. "Hana," he whispered, trying to get her to snap out of her funk. "Hana, can you hear me?"

Her lack of response remained firmly in place. Hana's thousand-yard stare offered no gateway to her thought process. In a way, it was probably for the best. Ivan was trying to check her coherence but had absolutely no idea what he could possibly say to her anyway.

***

Paula and Cindy sat back at their table looking a bit out of place amongst the other terrified guests. They had already been involved in the nasty celebratory "events" and were speckled and smeared in the bodily discharges of other participants.

They looked like hell because they'd gone through it. The horrid impacts would be infinite as showcased by the grim mood that was currently weighing them down. The girls had found a new plane of existence — one of utter ugly silence.

They had become warped backwards-world doppelgängers of their prior exuberance. They were still the same people that they'd always been, but now they projected the exact opposite emotion that had accompanied them to the party. Their cheerful, gossipy, fun-loving personas had been swapped out for a vibe of utter bleakness. There were no words that could've described their domineering dread.

***

In the bathroom, Lucas's stomach was still giving him issues. But the piercing stabs jabbing his abs were the least of his problems. Amid the sounds of mayhem, he'd finally found the courage to slither out from beneath the sink.

After scavenging the closet for something to protect himself with, he realized that there *was* no protecting himself. Hand soap and tissue weren't exactly viable weapons, even MacGyver wouldn't know what the fuck to do with that horseshit.

"C'mon, think! Think!" he said to himself.

He pulled the door open with impeccable caution, giving himself a minute sliver of window into the depravity he'd been imagining based on the sound effects echoing throughout the ballroom for the last few hours.

He could see Sebastian looking like a first-grader during nap time and the psycho jester watching over the flock of nervous survivors.

Lucas looked down at his dead cell phone that, on any other day, would have been the key to his escape. But on that cursed day, it was just a useless wad of alloy and circuitry. He gently closed the door and began to quietly ramble to himself.

"Any other fucking day," he said, slipping the inoperable device back into his front pocket. "They already searched in here… That sick fuck, Sebastian, sounded like he was prepared to die in this abortion of a wedding reception too. Maybe I can just wait them out. You just gotta wait them out, Lucas…"

***

Alyssa was physically shaking, so she moved her hands off of the table to avoid rattling the silverware and drawing any further attention to their table.

"What if we told him that he was in there? Maybe they would give us some kind of reward? Maybe it would be like a symbol of respect and they would let us live?" Sarah whispered, floating the idea of snitching on their coworker.

"How do you know Lucas isn't dead already? Just because he didn't come out of the bathroom doesn't mean the bullets he fired didn't go right into his fucking head," Alyssa retorted.

"Something tells me the creepy clown would have dragged him out here to at least show-off to Sebastian. Don't you think?"

"What kind of rat fink bitch are you, Sarah? That's our fuckin' friend in there and you're ready to just sell him down the river for a what-if," Keith scolded.

"Let's be frank, we all know Lucas is a selfish piece of shit. You're a goddamn sucker if you think he wouldn't sell you out in a heartbeat, Keith."

"Well, do you wanna talk to them? Because I sure as hell don't. Do you really think there's a better chance of them just letting us skip out of here merrily, or deciding that we're just gonna be part of the next sick ritual because we decided to interact with them like fucking idiots?" Alyssa clearly hated the idea but for different reasons than Keith.

"Not only that, haven't you seen Die Hard?" Keith interjected.

"Of course, I've seen fucking Die Hard, it's a classic," Sarah snarked.

"Do you wanna become Ellis? Because that's the road you're traveling down, sweetheart. Those terrorists scratched his ass out when he tried to play negotiator and these two whack-jobs seem a lot less stable than Hans Gruber."

"So, now we're using movies as the basis for our actions?" Sarah asked.

Alyssa slipped her hand back on top of the table and clenched the butterknife firmly.

"Keep your voice down! The fact is that drawing attention to us isn't gonna help. I'll tell you what, let me end the debate now. If you say one word, one fucking syllable that draws those maniacs over to our table, I'll find a way to force this flat tip through that precious neck of yours before you can even worry about trying to save it."

Keith was taken aback by Alyssa's overall savagery. He'd never seen her act so bold and sure about anything. It both scared and excited him.

"Do you understand me?" she asked, subtly pointing the silver at Sarah.

She watched Sarah nod her head, although it was obvious that there wasn't an inch of agreement between the two who were typically carbon copies of each other.

Alyssa exhaled a deep breath and lowered the utensil. "Good," she said as the word trembled from her chattering lips.

***

What if he knows all about me and Taylor? Seems like he knows everything else. But you can't have a party without music though, right? He needs me to some extent, I'm an asset to this sick ass game of his. At least for now I am… I need to find a way to keep it low-key and just hope I can survive a little bit longer than the rest of them, DJ Buttaz thought, looking at the still healthy number of guests sitting before his eyes.

He'd been sifting through the records for the relaxing shit, the music that might foster a tranquil atmosphere and keep his head attached to his shoulders and his guts inside his abdomen.

Happiness, romance, and slow-dance material were in a constant queue during Sebastian's nap time. Diana Ross, Lionel Richie, Sinatra, Elvis, and Stevie Wonder. He'd already gone through most of them. Loading them up like bullets into a gun but he was starting to run out of ammo.

Repeating the tunes was where insanity started, and things were already quite insane enough. The thought of redundancy didn't feel like a good move, but he was limited in the remaining options. He had no choice but to do what he always did and just play some fucking music.

***

All the faces around the table had been looking at Perry in the same way he felt like most people did throughout his life… like he was out of place. The fact that he was dressed like he was about to perform an oil change amongst the lavishly attired group didn't really help his cause for camouflage.

They probably think I'm drawing attention to us… they're probably right, he thought.

A short while ago, Perry tried to wipe most of the nasty jumble of gist and bone fragments off of his chair seat with his napkin. Much of the human slop had slowly slid down to the floor but the remainder of the grainy moisture had bled into the jumpsuit's posterior and down to his underwear. It had transitioned from warm and gross to cold and clammy while starting to congeal against him.

Perry was still trying to figure out exactly what was going on. Being a little late to the party, he'd had the questions lined up for some time, but his antisocial tendencies and general feeling of disdain toward his presence had been holding him back. The others hadn't said a word and it felt like someone needed to.

Fuck it, he thought.

"What happened? That guy looked so happy before…" Perry said, referencing the pleased image of the groom he'd witnessed in the hallway before everything had gone south.

A gentleman wearing a black bowtie looked at him, "In case you haven't noticed, he's gone mad. He's executing an incredibly thoughtful plan to exterminate all of us, or just about everyone… so he says."

"Why?"

"Apparently, it's the only goal he ever had in life. To kill as many people, as agonizingly slowly as anyone possibly could."

"Jesus…" Perry whispered, still in awe by the totality of the unsavory event.

"Never believed in him myself, but I think you're right. Only he can save us now…"

Perry racked his brain for an answer or any kind of direction. He wasn't really asking the man in the bowtie a question but it came out that way. "Where the hell do we go from here?"

"That one with the mask took all of our phones. Did you or the other staff you came in with, God rest their souls, have one?"

"No, he took all of ours too," Perry replied.

"So, they've put all of our contact with the outside world," the man paused, almost not believing what he was about to say, "they put it in that dunk tank filled with acid…"

The man glanced at them then back at Perry, "Now, it's just them and us. And make no mistake about it, they're in control."

"I see the gun, but we have them outnumbered, couldn't we just bum rush them?"

"Sure, you first," he replied smugly. "It's not just the machine gun, you see that," he pointed toward the enormous bomb on the bloody dancefloor.

Perry looked back slowly, and from the corner of his eye, he keyed in on it. The fat fluid tubes, the metallic infrastructure, and a jumble of multi-colored wires galore. It didn't take an explosives expert to understand what it was.

"He did a small-scale demonstration for us earlier," he continued, subtly pointing toward the destroyed table and human scramble of gore and extremities that was the children's table. "So, I'm guessing that one's the real deal. He's got it all triggered by a hand-activated control."

Perry's vision couldn't leave the face (or lack thereof) that was skinned down to the bone on one of the children. The exposed gums and teeth grinned back at him morbidly, leaving the tired old custodian unsure what to say next.

***

The steroid stable of fitness fanatics had been quiet for some time now. The earlier debates had died down and they all seemed to be waiting in angst for whatever came next. Whatever it was, they knew it wasn't going to be for the faint of heart.

"I can't believe we're gonna die here, all because of some bitch," Kwan said, holding back the same tears and whine for over an hour now.

"Of all the pussy in the entire world, we had to pick her," Luke mumbled in agreement.

"If this was only a fair fight, we'd mash that punk, Sebastian, and his goofy buddy," Rocky chimed in.

Brick remained mum, staring at Sebastian who was still laying on the stage but finally starting to awaken after his beauty sleep.

If what Rocky just suggested had the possibility of manifesting into reality, they would have all gladly accepted the challenge. What they didn't know was that, very soon, they were in fact about to get a shot at an impartial battle without fear of outside interference. Except, the opponents they'd be squaring off against weren't Sebastian and Jinx.

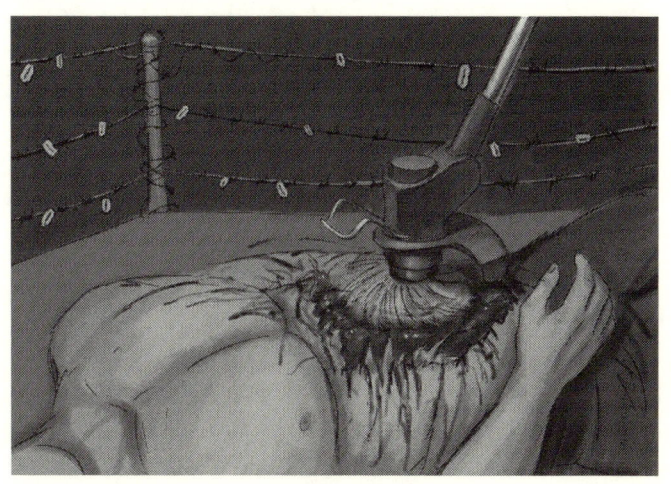

PILEDRIVER

Jinx sat at a small rectangular table they'd set up a few feet from the stage. In one hand, the jester held a miniature hammer which hovered above a bell that sat on the table. In the other hand, the jester held the AK-47 at the four speedo-clad brawny brutes on stage.

Each of the fellas had been forced to strip down to their birthday suits in front of the crowd and slip into the customized skimpy trunks that Sebastian had provided them. The fabric left little to the imagination; each pair was a different color and had the meathead's name spread across their buff posteriors.

Brick's trunks were the color of his name, Luke's were navy blue, Kwan's were jet black, and Rocky's were a smokey gray. They each had been given matching knee pads and either white or black lace-up boots that covered the majority of their calves.

Many of the meatheads wondered why they were dressed like professional wrestlers, but they were hardly surprised. Each of the men nervously stretched out their chiseled frames. As they warmed up, they understood that whatever ordeal they were about to get into would probably require them to be limber to survive.

Sebastian stood at the other end of the stage holding a cloth rope attached to the curtain while the crowd looked on with morbid curiosity. The sweat pumped out from his head and drizzled all over his collar. The veins popped in his neck while an unmistakable madness hugged his face. He cleared his throat and spoke bombastically and with more bass in his voice box than ever before.

"Tonight, we are going to witness the most anticipated match in the history of professional wrestling… for the heavyweight championship of the world!"

He waited a moment before continuing, "Well, not really… but it's the best we've got. But just to keep it interesting, we can make it for that gift there instead," he said, pointing to a carefully wrapped box that sat on the lip of the stage.

He cleared his throat a second time and opened his eyes, looking out toward his guests, "ARE YOU READY?!" he screamed.

The crowd half-cheered, not knowing exactly what kind of response he was looking for.

"I SAID, ARE YOU RRRRRRRRREADY?!"

The audience let out a roar that was loud but sounded like it was comprised of dozens of death whimpers in an effort to unlock the reaction that Sebastian's madness desired.

"Ladies and gentlemen, for the hundreds in attendance and the millions around the world that will never know. LLLLLLLLET'S GET READY TO RUMBLEEEEEEEEEEEEEEE!"

Sebastian turned back to the curtain and jerked the cord with brute force until the entire cloth had been pulled aside. Based on his introduction and the attire that the meatheads were currently wearing, what was revealed aligned perfectly.

The wrestling ring was no typical squared circle. Instead of the standard three ropes that normally encompassed the sizable perimeter, they had each been exchanged for triple knotted lengths of razor wire. Additionally, the four corners of the ring that were usually occupied by three padded turnbuckles had been replaced with a multitude of jagged glass shards and nails pointing outward.

A lone pair of steps allowed access into the ring and the floor outside was covered entirely with long modified beds of nails. The lethal foot-long spikes surrounded the entire ring, ensuring that anyone who was tossed over the top rope would be impaled by the ruthless metal and left to bleed out in agony.

Back inside the ring, there was a buffet of sadistic instruments. The harmful and warped weaponry included syringes, a cheese grater, cattle prod, a shopping cart, a fire extinguisher, and even a gas-operated weed whacker.

The eyeballs of the freshly anointed competitors grew lidless and a cutting fear crept inside each of them. Despite their lack of basic intellect, the boys understood what was fast approaching. Instincts gripped them as their flimsy friendships suddenly seemed irrelevant and forgotten. Continuing their warm-ups, they began to space out a bit and started sizing each other up.

"You're probably wondering how we pulled this thing off, but let me tell you, this place has worse security than the fuckin' Mandalay Bay!" he laughed heartlessly at his fanboy mass murder reference.

Sebastian activated a switch behind the curtain that turned on lighting in the rafters, illuminating the twisted theater of violence they were set to do battle in. He then took center stage and looked out to the people who were squirming with worry.

"In this four-man battle royal, the only way to win is to eliminate all of your opponents over the top rope. Only then will the champion be crowned and allowed to open their gift. At the sound of the bell, we'll be underway, and anything goes! DJ Buttaz, hit the music!"

DJ Buttaz put the most hype shit to the needle that he could find. He did his best to appease Sebastian, otherwise, he knew his own fate may be even worse than what was in store for the strong men on stage.

"Entering the ring first, named after construction material and the color he leaves leaking from his opponent's bodies... he is BBBBBBBBBBBrick!"

Brick looked a little confused but when Sebastian gave the hand gesture, he carefully trotted up the steel steps and worked his way between the razor wire and avoided making contact.

"Next, we have a toned foreigner who makes all the honey's hearts throb, sleeping in the basement of Gold's Gym, Kwwwwwwwannnnnnn!"

He gave him a nod and Kwan did as he was instructed, ascending the steps with grave terror unmistakably encapsulated in his expression.

"Heading in now, a man with the strength of ten oxen, and about the same wit. He is the modern-day Lou Ferrigno, misspelled but sounding the same... LLLLLLLLLLLLLUKE!"

Luke raced inside with his adrenaline pumping, preparing to fight the men he'd spent most of his days with. He was a little too excited. As he stepped through the razor ropes, his tense shoulders didn't get low enough and the metallic shredding steel raked across his massive bronze back.

"Agggghhhhhh!" he shrieked, falling down to the mat as blood began to gush from the ripped patch of flesh that let his insides show.

The other men looked shocked when they saw what would be the first blood of the contest.

"And last, but not least, with fists as hard as a boulder and also the mental capacity of one, he is the cynical stud, throwing shots as heavy as a two-week buzz, ROCKYYYYYYYYYYYYYYY!"

As Rocky stepped up, he knew he needed to be more cautious when entering the ring than Luke's dumb ass. But that thought was in the back of his mind. Primarily, he couldn't stop thinking about how much Sebastian knew about them.

He had a secret, one that he kept so close to the vest that even the three men in the ring never knew. Rocky was a huge fan of wrestling, something that the other three tended to ridicule and poke fun at.

Regardless of their feelings toward the offbeat form of entertainment, Rocky watched it religiously and had even been training with a retired former ring legend by the name of Madman Moses twice a week. The hardened veteran showed him a few things when he could catch him on a sober day.

It had progressed to the point where Rocky was scheduled to make his indie debut the following month. But his official inauguration would come sooner than expected and not with the well-thought-out measures taken beforehand. Rocky's first match would most likely be his last...

Sebastian watched each of the nervous men trying to keep loose in their corners. They had no words for each other, only a mixture of fear and dread in each of their pupils. Sebastian grinned and turned to the audience. "You're welcome," he said, pointing to Jinx who immediately dropped the hammer down three times on the bell.

Kwan looked the most nervous, grabbing hold of the handle of the shopping cart and pushing it forward gently as if trying to keep a bit of distance between him and the other competitors.

Rocky keyed in on him. It turned out the little dick jokes, racist cracks, and other frequent stinging jabs he constantly took at him weren't just playful locker room banter. Something about Kwan legitimately annoyed him. He couldn't really understand what, but either way, he wasn't ready to die, and thus took hold of the cattle prod laying on the mat a few feet away.

"I never really fuckin' liked ya anyway," Rocky mumbled, looking at his frightened friend.

Brick and Luke were both a bit shocked by his true feelings. But slowly, the surprise on their faces contorted as they each searched for anything they could to motivate enough hatred to fuel a murder.

They weren't quite ready to fight but they were trying to figure out a way to get there.

Meanwhile, Rocky needed no extra thoughts to proceed. He noticed that the handles of the metal shopping cart didn't have the plastic handguard that the grocery store normally did. Rocky's cagey observation revealed the whole carriage for what it was — a conduit to the *real* first blood.

Rocky activated the cattle prod and stuck it against the front of the cart that Kwan was so feebly trying to protect himself with. The wave of voltage was so overpowering that it froze him in place and caused him to gyrate violently.

With Kwan stunned, Rocky pulled back on the electroshock and kicked the cart, causing it to fall over onto its side in the middle of the ring. Then he put the boots to Kwan's solid abs, launching him back-first into the glass shards and rusty nails that peppered the corner turnbuckle.

As the ruthless combination of Sebastian's sadistic ingenuity tore into his screaming friend's bare back, he pushed down on his pec muscles, sending him deeper into anguish. Rocky jolted him one more time with the Taser before pulling him off of the spikes and synching his arms around his waist.

The polished snap on the belly-to-belly suplex launched Rocky's bleeding buddy over his head and saw the small of his back connect first with the base of the shopping cart. Kwan cried out again and laid motionless and gushing on the mat.

Brick was horrified by the violence that Rocky had unleashed on Kwan, and so was Luke. Except, Luke was so disturbed that he made it a point not to let it happen to him.

While Brick was focused in on the action, Luke had discreetly gotten hold of a pair of the syringes with the mysterious substance inside them and decided it was time to make his move.

He pounced on Brick, sticking both of the needle tips into the cheeks of his face and pushing down on the plungers immediately. Whatever was inside them wasn't friendly toward a human host.

Brick took a step back into the razor-wire rope screaming. As the slices reddened his skin, he placed both hands on his face. Almost right away, it had started to balloon. His cheeks pushed outward until the skin closest to the puncture holes started to come undone. The melt of human essence puked outward from his skull and left his hands collecting a bloody bubbling broth as it drizzled off the bone.

Brick fell to the foundation, shaking and losing control of his bowels. Like an abused dog relieving himself in extreme stress.

Luke was taken aback by what he'd done; the viciousness was too much. He didn't really know what he was expecting, maybe it was to survive, but what he'd done seemed far worse than just trying to hang in there.

Had he been as heartless as Rocky, he probably would've started up the weed whacker already, but instead, his hesitation left the device coming at his belly. The whipping plastic shredded Luke's gut.

The reoccurring theme of the crowd looking on in horror had no exception in this instance. They watched as the skin particles and tissue were knocked off of the muscle man's overly disciplined physique. His body's division looked like sweat flying off a boxer's scalp when he got struck with a knockout blow, or dust coming off an old shelf that had a slightly red tint. Luke watched on, and with each rotation of the whacker, a little more of him went missing.

The unexpectedness of the strike quickly sent Luke stumbling backwards into the razor-wire. His stomach looked like it'd received hundreds of mini corporal punishment lashes. The speed in which he back-stepped allowed the pointy steel to sink deep into his flesh. His arms flailed upward and curled around the ropes as the metal bit into his armpits.

Luke jerked his brawny body uselessly but he was now fully entangled. Rocky didn't wait to elevate the whacker blade to his face. The shredding lines of chaos burrowed into his nose and lips. It only took a few seconds to uncover his entire nasal cavity and leave his lips hanging off his face like wet mashed nightcrawlers.

Still snagged like a worm on a hook, Luke had stopped moving from the agony it caused. He sounded like a motor boat trying to plead for mercy liplessly to his dear friend.

Rocky wasn't having it and again pounced on the glaring opportunity, looking to finish him fast. He took a few steps away from Luke and cocked back the weed whacker. The big boy dashed forward and swung it with everything he had in the tank, like he was about to clothesline him with a baseball bat.

The steel arm connected under Luke's chin with such meathead force that it snapped in half and sent him toppling backwards over the top rope. Rocky pushed him forward for good measure and listened to the sickening rip of the flesh being detached from

141

his previously intertwined underarms.

Two juicy hunks of humanity were left hanging on the spiky rope as Luke fell belly-first onto the tall bed of nails below. The long spike impaled its way through his vital organs and exited numerous areas of his back and legs.

A gurgling noise could be heard as his motionless frame lost all movement, but Rocky wasn't waiting to bask in the glory. He knew that the deathmatch was far from over still.

While he understood the urgency of the situation, a small part of him kept yelling in his mind; *get your shit in.* The things that Madman had taught him couldn't go to waste. With Brick's head liquifying in the corner, and Luke already done for, Rocky wanted to put on a show. It was probably the only opportunity he'd get a chance to.

Rocky tossed the busted gardening device out of the ring and sized up Kwan. He was finally working his way back to his feet, but was favoring his back and his eyes were tight with anguish.

As Kwan saw Rocky barreling down on him, he was helpless. The forceful dropkick sent him flying into the barbwire. It ripped into his back, leaving flaps of skin fluttering. As he pulled himself away, Rocky was already standing up and waiting with the next spot in the deathmatch keyed up.

Seeing the glimmering cheese grater on the mat, Rocky realized the opportunity to have a little fun. He took Kwan's head into his armpit and yanked him down to the mat DDTing him head-first onto the cheese grater.

Kwan's forehead hit the unforgiving steel and the many sharp edges pushed his skin through the tiny holes, leaving hearty chunks of his cranium oozing and wedged inside.

The device had sliced into the back of Rocky's triceps too, but he enjoyed getting opened up a little. He shot to his feet quickly and removed some of the blood from his arm and smeared it like war-paint over his face and chest.

As Rocky stared out at the mortified crowd, screaming like Madman had taught him, he couldn't figure out why he wasn't getting over. He clearly wasn't the babyface he'd envisioned himself as, but that was no worry to him. He was happy to shift into a heel turn for the ages.

He picked up the already gory and dented cheese grater along with Kwan's limp head and looked out at the crowd.

"HOW IS THIS SHIT NOT GREAT TO YOU MORONS?! I KNOW WHY! IT'S BECAUSE NONE OF YOU JABRONIES KNOWS WHAT GREAT IS! YOU WOULDN'T KNOW, EVEN IF IT SMACKED YOU RIGHT IN YOUR UGLY FACES! I'LL SHOW YOU GREAT!" he said, holding up the bloody cheese grater like it was a relic passed on to him by God himself.

He brought his pathetic promo pun to life as he mashed the shredding steel into Kwan's already busted open face. As the crowd grumbled in discomfort, he raked the kitchen utensil back and forth over the exposed meat, shaving it off slowly while he screamed in a deranged manner.

Kwan was too concussed from the prior offense to scream along with him. As the blood rained down his nose and mouth, Rocky elevated his now nearly incapacitated friend to his feet and tossed the cheese grater aside.

He bent Kwan over towards him and stuck his gushing head between his legs and looked out over the top rope toward the crowd as if saying, 'I want you to see this nice and clear.'

Rocky hoisted Kwan up in powerbomb fashion but, instead, leveraged his incredible strength and allowed Kwan's mammoth frame to slowly slide behind him. Then he carefully hooked his hands under Kwan's armpits while keeping him elevated. As Kwan's lifeless body laid back-to-back with Rocky, he used all of his power to elevate him high over his head.

The Razor's Edge was an incredibly difficult and taxing move and was typically not performed when tossing the opponent over the top rope. It was dangerous enough to kill someone without the bed of nails on the outside of the ring, but nonetheless, that is where Rocky's eyes were aimed. In this one unlikely circumstance, it was horribly perfect.

Rocky launched him into the air back-first over the top rope. His brawny assets allowed him to vault the meaty bastard into the air about another foot or so. In total, the distance between Kwan and the nails was about seven or eight feet.

As Kwan's tattered and torn frame came down at breakneck speed, the onlookers knew it was going to be a rough landing. They gasped as the girthy spikes crushed through his once pristine bones and flesh. First, they pierced his wheezing lungs, and then punched a hole of violence through his rapidly pumping heart.

Maybe the most gruesome of the nightmarish injuries were the pair of girthy spikes that had lined up perfectly with each of his eyeballs and blasted through the back of his skull. It was like a cheesy B-movie that you saw back in the day in 3D how his eyeballs were left projecting outward with the gory orbs occupying the end of each spike. The rest of his head was driven backwards by the force of his motion, and his brain tissue slimed the rusty steel that had already run its way through him.

Expecting the roar of the crowd, Rocky threw his arms up. There was nothing offered to him. The best he could get was a gander at the slimy smirk on Sebastian's face and the blank and expressionless nothingness of his disturbed comrade still waiting to ring the bell.

"FUCK IT THEN! I'LL FINISH IT!" he grumbled, turning his way toward the final faceless bastard.

Rocky had gotten too cocky in believing that Brick's melting head had no wherewithal left in it. On a good day, it was rare, but on a bad day, it seemed impossible. But that day had already championed a lot of firsts.

Somehow, in all his runny glory, Brick had gotten his hands on the fire extinguisher. Just as Rocky turned around, he activated it and let a smog cloud of cold frost out toward Rocky's eyes.

Temporarily blinded, Rocky staggered about the ring punching at air while Brick wiped the blood out of his eyes and took aim. He charged him like a ram fighting for the right to deflower the prettiest in the herd and speared him with the extinguisher held out in front of his chest.

The impact of the blow was so powerful that when Rocky's shoulders connected with the top rope, it was too much. The poorly placed steel unfastened from the turnbuckle and the big son of a bitch flipped backwards out of the ring.

There was too much blood in his eyes for Brick to see exactly what happened to Rocky but he heard it quite clear. The squishy tissue tearing and ripping as the pointed bed penetrated his hulking physique upon awkward landing. The last gasps and gurgling blood running were music to his ears. But more important than anything else, the sound of the hammer cracking against the bell and it ringing out three times in a row let him know it was real.

"RING THE FUCKING BELL!" Sebastian screamed. "And here is your winner! BBBBBrick!" The PA system bellowed out with Sebastian's hyper enthusiasm.

He gestured to Jinx, and without exchanging a word, the strange jester left the table and slung the AK-47 behind his back. The demonic helper skipped to the stage and up the lone set of diamond-plate steel steps that were at ringside.

Jinx entered the ring and slowly guided Brick out of it as carefully as possible. With Brick's face looking more like a bowl of melting fruit-flavored ice cream, he would need assistance to seek out his reward. Jinx led him down until Brick's shaking legs gave way and he found himself kneeling in front of the pink mysterious box that contained his gift.

"Go ahead, big fella, have at it. That's all for you," Sebastian said.

Brick was in no condition to do his Christmas morning impression. He'd only received one strike in the match but it was a potato, and arguably the most devastating chess move to transpire amongst the four of them.

His cheeks, mouth, and chin area had dissolved down to the bone, showing off his glistening crimson skull exterior and lipless massive choppers. He fell over with his teeth chattering and his arms wrapped around himself like a child.

"Well, it's not really fun if I open it... but I suppose we don't have a choice," Sebastian said, shrugging his shoulders at the audience.

"I suppose it was a bit of a gag gift anyhow," he said, tearing into the perfectly wrapped packaging. "It's not for you but it's *for* you, you know what I mean?"

Brick couldn't respond, he was too busy starting to defecate all over himself. He couldn't even focus enough to watch as Sebastian extracted the wireless nail gun and squat over his trembling body.

"Seeing as you nailed my wife so many times, I think it's only fair that I get an opportunity to nail you too, wouldn't you say?" he asked Brick as he was just about finished shitting one.

He pressed the gun up to the exposed area of his face and started there. The nails traveled into the bone, sending shockwaves down Brick's body with each shot. He moved onto the teeth and pressed down hard. When the nail launched from the gun, it blew out the tooth and sent it flying down his hatch along with the pointed metal.

As Brick gagged and began to regurgitate the parts of his face and sharp steel he'd swallowed, Sebastian worked his way down to his abdomen and continued punching the nails into his guts. When the fast-moving spike rode through his intestinal tract, the additional pressure on his stomach helped further motivate the flood of feces that was now leaking out the edges of his wrestling speedo.

Like a lethal legion of ants, the nail trail started on Brick's face and trickled down his chest until Sebastian was left staring at his steroid-shrunken junk. He used the tip of the gun to feel around for his cock amongst the moat of rancid brown that secreted out of his overinflated trunks. Once Sebastian had located it, he aligned the end of the nail gun over the tip of his dick.

"It took a little while, but I think I finally found the wood," he laughed.

Another blast of hard steel punctured through his speedo and into the head of his cock, pinning it to his pelvis. Blood and excrement exited the front of his speedo as Brick squirmed in crippling pain.

Sebastian looked back around at Taylor who sat with an expression of defeat on her face; like she'd been homeless and beat down for decades. He'd almost forgotten about his bride since he was so involved in the match, but once it had concluded, he remembered the point of it.

"Sorry, honey, this sausage is smoked. I'm not sure you'll be able to snap into this Slim Jim ever again," he joked with a crinkle in his brow.

The madman sent three more nails out from the end of the device and into Brick. The shots followed down from the shaft and into his balls. With each potentially lethal injection, his runny secretions erupted upward into Sebastian's mug.

Heavily speckled with crimson and excrement, he rose the handle of the nail gun above his head and drove the weighty tool down with all his force. The metal unit fractured the already exposed skull and Sebastian watched the bone crumble before his eyes.

Sebastian continued to work on Brick's head but targeted the brain now. "Baby," he said, again trying to gain his wife's attention, "this Brick is one hard-headed mother fucker!" he bellowed out. "No pun intended..."

His relentless pounding eventually mashed the resilient dome as easily as an over-boiled potato. The body that he'd taken such scrupulous care of had been desecrated, along with the rest of his buddies.

Sebastian dropped the nail gun at the side of Brick's corpse while it gave off a finale of shudders, then walked back toward the curtain rope. He pulled it once again, this time, closing the curtain on the thoughtfully crafted death and mayhem that had been left on the stage.

Taylor and the rest of the spectators wished that making the horror vanish meant that it didn't happen. But even though a curtain was obstructing their view, they knew it was real. Besides, even with the curtain closed, there were still plenty of dead folks and other body parts sprinkled elsewhere in plain sight.

Sebastian took a tired look back at the crowd. Even he seemed to be getting a bit exhausted by the constant adrenaline surges and high tension.

"Show's over," he muttered.

A TOAST

Uncle Ivan had grown quite nervous, not just for his family but also for himself. That pesky little slip of paper sitting in his pocket had much more relevance than he'd initially thought. He knew there was a dark reasoning, some kind of sinister ulterior motive behind Sebastian having selected him to be the best man now.

He'd joked about it with his younger brother before Sebastian had his mood shift that led to his sibling's slaughter. He didn't know when, but he knew that, at some point, he would be called upon to give his speech. It was like knowing that doomsday was lurking just around the corner.

Only serving to further accelerate his fears was that amid the short intermission, his deranged nephew hadn't blinked. He'd been sitting at the edge of the stage and just staring him down; sockets gaping with frenzy and uncertainty.

What in God's name is he thinking? Cannot be good things. But what can I do? He remains in control at all times... he thought dejectedly, staring at the bomb and then back at the machine gun while still racking his brain to find a way out.

Sebastian finally stood up and walked away from the stage. He approached DJ Buttaz and retrieved the hand-held mic once again. He clipped it into the black microphone stand on the blood-drenched dancefloor and dragged it over to the table. He placed it where what was left of his fractured family remained seated and winked at his Uncle Ivan.

Sebastian then returned back to where he'd been standing and looked at the still sizable crowd. He snatched a glass and butter knife off of one of the nearby tables and returned to the mic.

Trepidation slammed around Uncle Ivan's belly as an uncanny instinctual sensation overcame him. His mouth dried up and his ticker raced faster than it ever had before. It was coming, he could feel it...

Sebastian smacked the edge of the knife against the glass gently. The normally exciting chiming noise was almost deafening in such a silent fear-stricken environment.

"It's time for a toast," Sebastian said, cracking a mischievous grin. He turned his head back toward his family. "Uncle Ivan, please," he said, pointing at the microphone.

Both Olga and Nina looked at him with eyes that begged him to stay seated, but realistically, they both fully understood that it couldn't happen. They wanted to cry, holler, and pull him down. They wanted to force him to stay, but they knew that would probably just get everyone killed.

Uncle Ivan approached the microphone stand. It was at the far end of their table, a few yards away from Uncle Ivan's wife and daughter, and right smack beside his still bewildered and traumatized sister-in-law.

Hana hadn't uttered a single word since the killing started. She looked like a mental patient who had been tortured and lobotomized then left to rot in an asylum for the rest of time. Witnessing her son's dark metamorphosis had broken her. She simply wasn't there anymore…

Jinx set a nearly full champagne bottle and a napkin down on the table beside Sebastian. Then the jester brought a long fancy candle and placed it beside the bottle. As Jinx lit the wick, the glowing flame added a hint of elegance to the table that was otherwise covered obnoxiously in bodily splatter.

"Ladies and gentlemen, it's time for the best man to say a few words!" It seemed Sebastian had found his enthusiasm again.

Uncle Ivan's hands shook as he removed the wrinkly folded piece of paper from his interior suit pocket. When he unfolded it, his wrinkly hands shook uncontrollably like he had Parkinson's disease. What does one say at the wedding of a recently christened prolific mass murderer?

"But before you get started, I think I wanna tell a little story if that's alright… Is that alright with everyone?" Sebastian asked.

The crowd grumbled their many approvals half-heartedly, knowing damn well they had little other choice in the matter.

"I'm incredibly grateful to each and every one of you for being here. Maybe I haven't truly made that clear but the sacrifice that you're all making is truly appreciated and something special." Emotion began to overcome him.

"You know… I didn't know if this day would ever actually happen. I didn't know if it would come. For years, I'd been ready but I wasn't going to go through with it unless every tiny detail was just right. There were a lot of dark and empty nights, depression, some tough times on a bumpy road to find my opportunity."

Sebastian looked back at Taylor, "But then I met my wife…" he was choking up, tears ran down his cheeks. "Love you, honey," he smiled madly, sending a fluttering wave in her direction. "Sure, I'd found someone that was perfect, someone that just really truly deserved it…"

Taylor subtly crinkled her brow at him as if what he was saying was total fabrication.

"Even then though, I still wasn't sure… until this place reopened that is. *That* was a sign from the universe. *That* was something telling me this was all supposed to go down this way. Many of you outside of my immediate family might not know, but this hotel holds a very special place in my heart."

Sebastian pointed his arm out at the lovely arching windows and the mountains that were now dimly lit and on the verge of nightfall.

"We used to go skiing here when I was just a kid. Back when it was still open anyway. I always loved this place because I got to be around so many people. Even as a young man, I wanted to do something special like this for a long time."

He wiped the teardrop treads away from his face and tried to compose himself.

"I'm glad I waited, though, because nothing, and I mean NOTHING, could be better than today. But decades ago, I almost screwed all this up. I got greedy and tried to rush it."

He looked out the window, playing the memory over in his head. While disgust crinkled his face, there was still a fondness that fluttered in his heart regarding the vision.

"The last time we stayed here, I snuck out of my room in the middle of the night. I eventually made my way to the kitchen, but it wasn't because I was looking for a midnight snack, I assure you..."

Sebastian finished what remained in his glass and set it down on the table.

"After a day of snooping around away from the slopes, I'd discovered that the hotel had a bit of a rat problem. This was evident when I located a variety of different poisons they'd been using in an effort to kill off the vermin population. The supply closet I stumbled upon would have been an exterminator's wet dream. It excited me too. However, it had never been small pests that I'd been interested in exterminating."

He giggled childishly recalling the silly times of his adolescence. "You see, even at such a tender age that gave my tiny brain a devilish idea, and so I set off to find the waffle batter. I'd had the continental breakfast what felt like a million times before. The sausages were always awesome, and the spread they set up allowed people to hand-make their own waffles in that fancy cooker. You remember, right, Mom? We always loved it!"

Hana remained stoic and without movement.

"Anyway, I'd seen at least a hundred or so people get fed every time I was there. I watched that little line of death stand happily while salivating. Getting ready for that hot and crispy golden-brown waffle to hit their mouth. At least I thought it was a line of death at the time…"

Sebastian looked a little embarrassed sharing his confession with everyone, knowing that his initial attempt at mass murder was mostly a failure.

"That was my chance, and I took it. But it wasn't well-thought-out. Only several elderly folks who attended the breakfast actually died. Nope, that shitty rat poison wasn't quite strong enough to get the job done against the young and healthy. And that, ladies and gentlemen, is why they closed this place… They couldn't survive the onslaught of grief and lawsuits that hit afterwards, so they just shut the fucking doors instead."

Sebastian looked away from the crowd and over toward his mother. Hana's jaw was chattering like she wanted to say something, but nothing ever seemed to come out.

"I guess it's a good thing no one had a hankering for waffles that morning, huh, Mom?" Sebastian said with a detached laugh.

"YOU MONSTER!" Hana finally bellowed out, triggered by the memories of years past. "You're not my son, you're a demon!" she screamed.

Sebastian picked up the napkin from the table beside him and stuffed it into the champagne bottle.

"I hate you! I hate you, demon!" she continued.

Uncle Ivan, unsure of exactly what to do, turned to her and tried to calm her.

"If I'm a fuckin' demon, and you're the one who created me…" he said, sticking the napkin into the lit candle. It caught fire, suddenly revealing that it wasn't actually a celebratory champagne inside the bottle, it was gasoline. "Then shouldn't you burn in hell too?!" he screamed, launching the smoking Molotov cocktail at his mother.

The jade glass shattered over Hana's face and engulfed both her and indirectly Uncle Ivan in hot flames and accelerant. They fell backwards while Olga and Nina simultaneously shrieked in horror.

Hana fell over and tried to think straight but it was difficult with her entire exterior on fire. Once she was able to deter her focus from the scorching pain and get her brain working, she got an idea. It was the only thing that made sense to her. If she was going to die, Sebastian needed to go with her.

She charged him with the hope that she could simply wrap her arms around her son and let them both burn to ashes. With her arms outstretched and her feet driving her forward, it was all she had left to achieve. But the cluster of bullets that left the banana clip tore through her flaming flesh before she ever had a chance to reach Sebastian.

As Jinx squeezed down on the trigger, blood and orange pushed out of her skin. She fell into the messy pool of people on the dancefloor as the little life that remained drained out.

Jinx had the fire extinguisher from the wrestling match on standby and ran over toward Sebastian's flaming mother.

"Don't! Let them burn, the fire alarms are deactivated already. Just put out the fire on the chair and table," Sebastian instructed.

As Uncle Ivan fell to the floor screaming, he tried the stop, drop, and roll method. Unfortunately, it did zero to stop his flesh from continuing to bubble and blister. His family watched on in repulsion as the man of the house was roasted like a pig.

Sebastian grinned and looked out at the stunned crowd. "I guess now we'll never know what he was going to say..." he chuckled, looking down at his Uncle Ivan who was still being eaten away by the flames but no longer moving.

BOUQUET
BLOODBATH

Jinx had just finished pulling all of the bodies off the dancefloor and making space. The pile of disfigured corpses and limbs was stacked up on the right side of the stage and helped free up a sizable area. The normally pristine wooden surface still looked like a human oil slick, but it would have to do.

Sebastian finished unwrapping another gift to himself and brought the Ruger 9mm over to the dancefloor with him. The box also contained dozens of clips, one of which he immediately inserted.

"Alright, I'm having a damn good time, but we gotta speed things up. It's getting dark outside and I'm sure there's a lot of people who love and miss you guys. People who are going to soon start wondering where the fuck you are in a few more hours. So, let's start with the ladies…"

Sebastian turned back to Taylor who was still sitting beside her gruesomely mutilated family members. "Honey, if I could just have you join me up here, I know this one is something that you've been pretty darn excited about," he smiled.

Sebastian fixed his sights to the wall on the other side of the room. "And if I could please have all the gentlemen step off to the side. Just line up against the windows please, and don't worry, we'll be getting to you soon."

The small sea of people pried themselves away from each other, crying and saying their goodbyes. Many of them didn't want to leave each other, but in their hearts, they knew there wasn't much they could do. Whatever twisted idea Sebastian had in store for them they'd have to participate or face swift execution. Their only chance at survival was total obedience.

"Cindy, Paula," Sebastian said, locking onto the girls in the crowd. "You can both join the men. Since you've already competed earlier, I'm going to give you each a pass on this one."

The blood-drenched, deflated duo trotted over to the sideline, not any more joyous or depressed than they'd been moments before. It was as if they were dead inside already; just pretty mindless meat wandering around without a purpose.

Perry looked at the pair as they came to a stop just in front of the men, recalling the hell that they'd been through. They both looked like they would never be the same again. He wondered if that would be the case for himself.

While Perry was grateful that he wasn't going first, he knew the men were next. He eyeballed the lonely vacant bar salivating for the slightest form of escapism. The jittery janitor would have given his left nut to go over and fix himself a drink. *I need a goddamn drink, just a little something to take the edge off. I need to get away from this insanity. Why the hell did I have to come in today?*

Perry closed his eyes, moving on from his thirst. Instead, he pictured his quiet and boring apartment in his mind. The lights were out, the couch was old, the television was small, and the fridge was mostly bare. But the normally melancholic and always inconsequential room was the only place he wanted to be. If only he could tap his heels together three times and be teleported.

As outlandish as the sick day's events had been, Perry knew that was still a ridiculous idea. His shoes might've been red but not in the manufactured and garish way that Dorothy's were in the classic film. They were red from stepping through the hunks and reservoir of human filling that littered the ballroom. They were gory, not gaudy.

Perry found himself exiting his stupor while staring at the red glazing that coated his boots. Then, suddenly, the sound of Sebastian's voice echoing drew his attention back once again.

"The bouquet toss has been around for hundreds of years. The odd tradition supposedly took off in England where various guests attending a wedding would try to rip off a little piece of the bride's wedding gown or her flowers. The idea was that by stealing those items from the bride, the thief could somehow get her luck to rub off on them in the process. Then they too would be able to find both love and happiness…"

Sebastian carefully picked up a bouquet of extra thorny roses and looked at the mass gathering of terrified women. He handed the flowers to Taylor and she unknowingly grabbed them with a normal grip strength.

As the thorns unexpectedly plunged into her pores, she let go and whined under her breath. The vibrant red petals fell to the ground as her hot blood drizzled out all over them like a candy topping.

"Get those off the floor!" he screamed, lasering a dirty glare that could've burned a hole through her.

Taylor quickly used her leaky hands to lift up the bouquet, this time, much more cautiously. That thoughtfulness in handling them would mean nothing as Sebastian set his gun down on the table.

He gripped each side of his wife's hands and applied extreme pressure, crushing down on Taylor's palms and fingers. She cried out again as the thorns dug deep toward her skeleton and blood began to ooze rapidly. Her mitts were almost completely red now as the savage compression left fluid surging like Sebastian was juicing an orange.

"Don't let go of them again until I fucking tell you to…" he ordered.

Sebastian took his hands off Taylor's and twirled his maroon finger around. Taylor turned her back to the women as instructed and loosened her grip enough to unplug the thorns from the peppering of divots that littered her ravaged palms.

Sebastian then turned his attention back to the ladies. "Over the years, it evolved into what you see at most weddings today. A woman blindly tossing a cluster of flowers over her shoulder, and a bunch of her lonely friends battling it out playfully. But today will be a little different than the standard. Let me assure you, ladies, that there will be much more on the line than finding the right swinging dick to lay beside."

Sebastian looked over at his aunt, Olga, and his cousin, Nina, who remained still seated at their table. They were just a stone's throw away from Uncle Ivan's crispy corpse.

"Auntie, Nina, what the fuck are you waiting for? Get up! Neither of you are excluded from this exercise!" he screamed, picking up his gun again. "You're a widow now anyway, and trust me, at your age, you're gonna need a little luck with the fellas."

They each quickly scurried into the outskirts of the crowd. There must have been over a hundred girls all squished together. All frothing at the mouth to find a way to secure the precious bouquet that was undoubtedly about to get flung into the crowd. Those flowers were the extension of life, at least for a little while anyway…

"Now, I'm sure you've all seen videos, or maybe even witnessed it a time or two in person. The one-off viral occasions where girls during these silly little contests go completely batshit in their attempt to secure these stupid flowers. Well, I can tell you that whatever you've seen in the past, prepare to zip past it because, today, the last lady holding onto this thing will be the only one of you that gets to live."

A resounding horrified gasp let the wind out of nearly the entire room. Jinx loaded a fresh clip into the AK-47 and prepared a few others. The twisted jester was most certainly going to need them.

"It's gonna be kind of like a game of hot potato, except you're gonna wanna be holding the hot potato when it's all said and done. And if you don't all end up killing each other by the end of this thing, Jinx here will be ready to do some clean-up," he said, pointing to the deranged figure cocking the rifle.

"I'm going to set my watch for ten minutes. Feel free to duke it out on the dancefloor or utilize the cutlery at your tables, but under no circumstances should you leave those areas. If you do, these bullets promise you won't get far…" he cocked the hammer back and pulled the bomb detonator from his jacket.

"And don't forget, should you get any ideas as a group, I'll happily blow us all to holy hell," he reminded them smugly.

He looked at Jinx and smiled before repocketing the detonator. "Oh, one other thing. These flowers are going to get torn to shit, so just focus on keeping the stems. I've tied them together firmly. So, don't get caught up on rose petals laying on the floor, your goal is to be the last one with the stems stabbing into your hand. Okay, are you all ready?"

There wasn't a dry eye in the crowd of dread-filled females. Every last one was emotional and trying to prepare themselves to do whatever it was they were about to do. They were far from ready but had little choice in whether they'd be participating or not. They all understood that they were at the mercy of a maniac.

Sebastian looked at Taylor with an eagerness that you might see in a child waiting for the doors to open at the toy store. "Honey, let's make someone the second luckiest lady in the room," he said with a sickening wink.

Taylor didn't hesitate or feel the slightest bit of pity in tossing the bloody bouquet off into the pit of suddenly ghoulish girls. Since the slaughter of her family, she'd only been thinking about saving her own Jennifer Lopez caliber ass. Friends came and went; they were expendable. She could give a fuck less if all of those bitches tore each other to ribbons as long as she gave herself the best chance at strutting out victoriously in the end.

As the scarlet saturated flowers arched over Taylor's head and back to the small army of women, it felt like time had stopped. Their pretty raining eyes all saw the bouquet descend in slow motion. All the heartwarming and caring moments in their lives flashed as each woman prepared themselves for battle. Some by removing their high heels, others gritted their teeth, and most balled their fists.

A rainbow spectrum of endless fingernails burst upward toward the runny roses that were getting closer. As they entered the savage cluster, suddenly, the entire dancefloor snapped into a pinnacle of violence mirroring that of hardcore punk mosh pit when the chorus hits. White-knuckle fists swinging wildly but with even more reckless abandon — their fuel was entirely comprised of malicious intent.

DJ Buttaz had been sweating profusely while watching the scene unfold. He knew that their tormentor would want music to accompany the melee but Sebastian hadn't provided him with any instruction.

It was incredibly important to his survival that he chose something the maniac would enjoy being paired with the bloodshed. Despite being the most disturbed man he'd ever seen, DJ Buttaz also noticed that Sebastian seemed to have a sense of humor. Banking on those slivers of his comedic personality shining through, DJ Buttaz reached across the pond and put the needle to a record that read: THE BENNY HILL SHOW THEME SONG.

It was evident at once that the hilarity of the goofy soundtrack was not lost on Sebastian. He turned to DJ Buttaz and connected his thumb and index finger to make a circle that left the remaining three fingers held outstretched. The symbol of perfection and approval allowed the disc jockey to exhale a deep sigh of relief.

Meanwhile, on the dancefloor and in the dining area, the sentiment was the polar opposite. It didn't take any convincing for the ladies to be driven to violence. They had seen enough of the prior bouts to understand that if they weren't holding the bouquet when the time was up, it would not only be their last chance at love but their last chance at life.

The overall barbarity was primal; souls who, for the most part, had never so much as gotten in someone's face suddenly found themselves without morals. A gutted sensation ruined them as their hearts dropped into their bellies and everything they'd ever been taught was pushed aside.

The roses landed in the slender hand of a woman that the groom was quite familiar with. Sebastian had mentored Sarah for the last few months at work, but she wasn't thinking about that anymore. Sarah seemed well aware that no professional connection would serve as her salvation. She could only save herself moving forward.

As the sharp thorny stems slashed into her flesh, a merciless skirmish sparked all around her. It was like feeding time for a pack of rabid wolves. The circle of eager guests that surrounded her quickly swallowed her up. Press-on nails snapped as they ripped away pieces of her dress, clumps of hair, and flower petals, but Sarah didn't let go.

As a former high school basketball star, Sarah prided herself in keeping a well-maintained and sturdy physique. It was going to take more than some cat clawing and a few plucked follicles to stop her. Sarah pushed her way through the crowd of crazed girls like she was headed for a layup. They scraped at her skin and tugged her in different directions but none of them seemed stronger than her willpower.

Sarah trucked over a trio of frail elders who lined the perimeter of the chaos sphere and finally broke through. She quickly jumped on top of the vacated table that was closest to the wall. She'd kicked her heels off when the carnage had begun. It was a critical decision and allowed Sarah to use her feet to carefully land in the center of the tablecloth.

As the mob of floral junkies stood frothing mere yards away, she quickly analyzed the situation. There wasn't much to go on, but as the precious seconds ticked away and the sinister brigade closed in, she calculated a long shot.

Embedded along the wall above Sarah, about a foot taller than she stood, sat a rippled, decorative trim. It stretched the length of the wall and the meticulously carved wooden design came out about five inches. Just far enough that her toes might be able to gain some shaky footing. A short distance above the trim sat a masterfully painted gold-framed nature scene.

Sarah wished she could crawl into the oil canvas and escape the war behind her. She'd run past the trees and flow down the running stream to freedom. But the reality was, she needed to be both extraordinary and intelligent if she was to be the one left standing when the time ran out. Wishful thinking sure as hell wasn't going to keep her alive.

As the ravenous guests reached the table, in her mind, there was but one option. Sarah stuck the prickly flowers between her jaws and pinched down. She immediately felt the thorns pierce into her tongue and stab the corners of her mouth, but her hunger for survival motivated her to ignore the extreme discomfort.

As the oral agony and bleeding commenced, she vaulted off the tabletop and her fingers turned into ridged claws. She was by no means a mountaineer but had spent a Saturday afternoon in a rock-climbing gym. She internally praised herself for accepting the awkward first date suggestion from a random guy she'd met on the internet the year prior.

Sarah was thankful that the fixture looked to have been implemented during the initial design and not some chintzy add-on years later. It was sturdy and allowed her a firm foundation to pull herself up. But she would need a little help before she could accomplish that.

She stretched her right arm up and took hold of the corner of the massive painting. It was fixed tightly to the wall and able to remain attached while Sarah slid her knee up on the ornamental ledge. The pack of raging ladies below clawed at the frayed dark leggings that covered her feet. The pointed wicked nails missed her toes by mere inches as she pulled herself away from their malicious clutches.

As Sarah gained her balance, a glass full of water suddenly crashed into the artwork beside her. Next came a plate, and then various silverware. Their aim wasn't the best and some of the dinnerware didn't even come close.

"You throw like a bunch of fucking girls!" Sarah laughed. Her words sounded strange as her mouth was still gushing and it was difficult to speak with the cluster of stems still locked between her jaws.

A small group of disturbed women all tried to stand atop the table as Sarah had done, but they weren't quite the same tier of athlete as her. As three of them reached the tabletop at a sluggish pace, the weighty frame buckled, sending the well-dressed guests crashing down and onto plates of half-eaten food and a sparkling flowered centerpiece.

Seconds after, like a swarm of yellow-jackets, the other women began to make their way over. They somehow found the levelheadedness to collaborate their group bloodlust. They pushed the table and cloudy-minded girls in the middle of it aside.

Then, like some kind of bizarre cheerleading act, a few of them formed a foundation on their hands and knees. The women behind them jumped on their backs as the human pyramid began to form, inching closer and closer to Sarah.

Her eyes widened as the river of blood continued to drool down from her mouth. Her feet were planted firmly as best they could be on the ledge. Her right hand remained on the fauna portrait. The left one was affixed to another painting a few feet away of what looked to portray a British aristocrat.

Sarah's stability was anything but a sure thing.

She knew there was still probably plenty of time before the contest was up. Plenty of time for the unhinged women to get hold of her. As they closed in, she knew that she needed to make a move.

The ratty woman with raccoon streaks of mascara slithering down her face hoisted herself to the top of the carnal triangle to the encouragement of the desperate group.

"Get her! She took the flowers!" said one woman. "Pull her down so everyone has a fair chance!" screamed the next.

There was nothing fair about the entire evening and nothing fair about life in general. And there was certainly nothing fair about what Sarah did next.

She waited for the possessed lady to claw her way up until she was nearly at her shin level. But before she could gain her balance, the edge of Sarah's heel found her skull.

Sarah held onto the firmly fastened canvases as tight as she could to assist in her downward kick. The ratty woman hadn't even seen it coming. As she reached the pinnacle of mortal steps, Sarah's foot cracked her square on the button.

Her hand remained clasped around the woman she was supposed to be standing on, and as she fell downward, the entire spur of the moment awkward architecture toppled over.

The ratty woman landed head-first, the sound of her spine shattering would have been easy to hear had it not been for the psychotic chirps coming from the remaining women. They seemed frantic and frustrated that Sarah had outwitted the majority of the populous.

Sebastian watched on enjoying what he was

seeing but not quite enjoying it enough. He turned to Jinx, "She surprised me. Hasn't disobeyed the rules, yet somehow, she's found a way to make this more boring than it should be. Very clever, very resilient, very resourceful... Hell, that's why I hired her…"

The memory rushed back into his mind of her interview. How Sarah just knocked every question out of the park. She had the ability to adapt quickly and think fast. The fact that he'd offered her a job and managed the woman almost seemed like a distant dream from a past life.

"Under different circumstances, she'd be getting a raise for this, but instead, she's just pissing me off."

Unbeknownst to Sarah who was still trying to calculate her next move, Jinx aimed the AK-47 up at her torso in the distance. Upon hearing Sebastian's dismay, the sinister figure seemed motivated to assist however possible.

"No, not her. We can't punish her for doing what she's supposed to. Why don't you motivate the rest of them instead?" Sebastian stepped away and headed back to the presents as Jinx took aim into the swarm of scared women.

Olga and Nina had stayed out of the melee for the most part. Olga had no idea what to do but figured it might be best to strike toward the end. It didn't matter who was holding it in the moment, it was only relevant at the conclusion of Sebastian's selected time allotment.

She had done her best to keep a distance between them and the violence while fixing her gaze on the fancy hands of the grandfather clock against the far wall. Olga would know when the right moment to strike was. But as her sights drifted to Jinx hoisting the cannon and ready to release a violent volley of rapid-fire rounds, that moment certainly hadn't arrived.

As Sebastian's wicked helper pulled down on the trigger, the cracks of hot lead being projected into the ballroom rang out. Both Olga and Nina dove and disappeared under the long table cloth in front of them that was draped to the ground.

The gunfire tore cavernous gorges through the frenzy of elegant garments. The faces that had been artfully crafted with carefully applied cosmetic products couldn't hide the reality. Blood splattered upon them, faces lost their form, total hell had been unleashed.

From the other side of the room, the group of high-strung men standing like enslaved creatures watched on as the ladies they loved, the mothers of their children, were put down without a second thought. Exterminated like diseased cattle, as if it was just another day on the farm. And there wasn't a damn thing they could do about any of it.

The sickening screams sent chills up Perry's back, causing him to physically tremble. "This… it… it just can't be happening. Please, God, just let me get through this. Just help me find a way to stop them," he mumbled.

Perry had never been one to pray but that sort of behavior was the go-to in a situation that was so grim and fantastical. No mortal seemed to be in a position to whisk him away from the monumental massacre that he'd been forced to sit through.

But in reality, he knew there was no feasible way for him to stop or even temporarily pause the process without becoming another step in the slaughter. In reality, Perry knew that God would've showed up awhile before that moment if he was going to play hero.

"There's nothing you can do. Nothing any of us can do except try to win. They're holding all the cards, old man," Keith said to Perry while knowing he was most likely watching his coworker's final moments.

"You really think that these two are gonna let someone live?" His sarcastic tone implied that the murderous actions in front of them would seem to indicate otherwise.

"That's what he said. So, I guess that's the best we can hope for..." Keith replied.

Suddenly, the shooting stopped. Perry looked back at Jinx as the jester inserted another banana clip with the quickness and monotony of a factory line worker and got back to blasting.

Perry gritted his teeth and pinched his bottom lip with his discolored enamel. He watched the already dwindling crowd of beautiful ladies continue to die out. The ones that tried to run out of the contest area Jinx peppered first. The jester's accuracy would have been highly admirable if the shots weren't intended to explode the skeletal framework of countless innocent women.

The bodies were piling up once again. Perry watched Sarah remain frozen between the two paintings, trusting that she'd already have been dead if that was the intent behind the shooting.

Then his eyes drifted down to Alyssa, who had been very hesitant about the conflict the few times he'd watched her. She'd yet to mount the slightest offense and appeared shaken by the cruelty that surrounded her. He wondered if her timid approach was strategic or if she was just in the grasp of Medusa's panic—frozen in stone.

Perry's eyes then worked their way over to Taylor. She stood fearfully to the side of both Jinx and Sebastian. She was the definition of a hot mess. Her stunning beauty had intermingled with the horrors that unfolded. Blood still dribbled from her mouth and hands. Overall, based on the stains all over her gown, you would've thought she was an oil painter as opposed to a glamorous bride who had just been wed.

He shifted his vision back to the core of absolute chaos. Perry felt watching all these folks and how they responded might somehow help his cause. He felt a little guilty taking mental notes while people's lives were ending. He felt uncomfortable to admit it, but in a way, he was just like the rest of them; looking to gain the slightest edge on the competition. He knew he needed to do whatever he could to stay alive. Otherwise, his boring apartment would miss him.

A tiny smirk manifested as he thought about the simplicity and utter uselessness of his life. Maybe it was true, maybe he was replaceable and had barely made a dent in the universe. Or maybe most other people just thought they had a larger impact than they actually did. Either way, it didn't make one life more valuable than another.

Perry's eyes remained on Alyssa as she stayed low and watched Jinx. Suddenly, after more rounds grounded a pair of girls just a few feet away from her, she seemed extremely uncomfortable. The wine glasses and smooth bottles shattered above her head, motivating her to seek a firmer form of shelter. The only shelter available to her.

She looked into the one good eye and missing face of the gagging girl on the ground that she dove behind for cover. The bloody baseball slide put her too close for comfort as she stared into the gorge of hopeless horror.

It looked like someone had used an ice-cream scooper with a razor tip and dug out hearty chunks deep into the woman's eye socket and cheek. She laid her face down, on the verge of death, but that would do little for Alyssa's protection.

She pushed the desecrated girl's fractured outline up on her side and revealed an enormous exit wound in her abdominal area. As Alyssa listened to her death rattle, she grabbed the top of her dress and continued to look at what was left of the woman's ghastly face. She gritted her teeth and positioned her to use as a human shield.

With the lady in front of her and a few more bodies that had dropped around them, she felt safer than before but not by much. The girl looked like she was trying to communicate when Alyssa felt her body shake as the pair of slugs made impact.

The first hunk of hot metal burrowed into her backside and went through the dying woman, eventually finding its way into Alyssa's love handle. As she opened her mouth to scream in pain, the poor girl's already desecrated head came apart entirely. The bullet avoided passing through into Alyssa's head, but the gnarly warm and wet contents of the stranger's deepest thoughts were catapulted into her hatch for her to chew on.

She spat out as much of the woman's head as she could, choking while trying to tuck her face away from the gunfire. Still, Alyssa couldn't help but swallow some of the fragmented skull and felt the fractions of bone scraping against her esophagus en route to her belly.

Perry couldn't believe what he was watching. It was like an action movie and horror film rolled into one ferocious frame. While he was pulling for the girl, he was becoming a bit desensitized by the relentless mayhem. His eyes couldn't help but drift off of Alyssa and back over to Sebastian.

"What the hell are you doing now?" Perry asked, watching Sebastian drag another gift-wrapped object away from the stage.

Before Sebastian made his way back to the contest area, he became lost in thought. He watched in a state of suspended glee as the lethal shots rained down upon the helpless. Sebastian stood frozen in time as he watched the women drop. Massive holes blew through them, limbs were mangled, and lives were lost.

Ten became twenty, and then fifty, yet still, Jinx showed no signs of stopping. The heartless jester emptied clip after clip until there were more magazines laying around than a doctor's office. It only took a few more moments of rapid fire before Jinx had reached the cusp of a feminine genocide.

Sebastian peeked out at the array of violence and did his best to gather a quick count of the remaining ladies that had dodged the menacing waves of bullets with bad intentions. He seemed satisfied that about half a dozen or so remained breathing or free of critical wounds.

"Okay, that's enough, we need a few of them still," Sebastian said to Jinx before turning back to what remained of the ladies.

"Alright, sorry for the outburst, but in fairness, it was getting a little boring for us. So, I'm going to add something to the mix. This something is what got me through those lonely teenage years," Sebastian said, unwrapping the paper and tearing open the box.

He pulled out an aluminum Easton baseball bat that had more dents and dimples than the moon's surface. Some of the paint was worn in areas but it still seemed to be firmly intact. A baseball was bundled with it which he set down on the table.

"I killed more stray cats and neighborhood dogs with this fucking thing than neglect and cancer combined. She was a little pricey, but I had to get an aluminum one. Damn wooden ones just kept breaking on me. I guess I was a strong kid! Anyhow, whoever gets my precious bat here is gonna have quite the advantage," he smiled, still gazing fondly upon the instrument of anguish.

"Since you girls were all kind of loafing it before, I'm gonna forget what time it was and just set my watch for seven minutes. Seven is a lucky number." He winked at the gruesome girls that remained and pressed the button on the side of his timer.

"Now, have at it!" Sebastian yelled, tossing the bat up into the air.

Olga magically reappeared out from under the table she'd crawled beneath when the violence had started. It was time to make her move. Her vision searched for the metal stick but her ears found it faster as she heard it clink against the ground just a few feet beside her.

As Olga raced toward the weapon, Alyssa was the next closest person and leaped up like a bat out of hell. She forgot about the gunshot wound in her side and collided with Olga. But the force of Olga's stride was more powerful and able to knock Alyssa backwards. She fell down at Olga's feet, slipping in the crimson slick on the dance floor. Fortunately, to Alyssa's relief, she fell directly onto the steel.

She gripped it tightly like she'd never heard or understood the concept of compassion. She brought the steel stick backward, and just as Olga was gaining her footing, the MLB-worthy swing smashed into her skull. The doink noise of the tin being struck against bone echoed in the room, causing many of the men observing to wince and cringe.

Olga tumbled over with her eyes still open but her consciousness had escaped them. Her cracked cranium was split wide open within her hairline, and her already mashed head landed hard on the bloody wooden floor. She laid motionless and bleeding by a severed foot wedged inside a red-specked high heel.

The otherwise pretty foot had been severed or maybe blown off from the prior rampage and activities. The area was an utter mess but Alyssa was ready to make it even messier. She raised the bat up again and drove it down with crushing speed. Like a shark smelling blood in the water, she further extended the gape in her head until her brain tissue was exposed under the elegant light of the chandelier.

"Six minutes!" Sebastian yelled, enjoying what he was seeing but reminding her she needed to keep up the pace.

Alyssa heard the footsteps of the three other girls running up on her. They had decided to try and overpower her but were not nearly as strong or cagey as they thought. Alyssa felt a newfound darkness throbbing inside her as she swung the bat, connecting directly with the first one's jawbone.

The force of the vicious blow cracked her hinge and launched a plethora of her pearly whites off into the distance. The once vital and downright attractive consumption mechanism now uselessly hung off her face in a ghoulish manner. She landed hard with her eyes shut—mouth chattering like a gossip girl.

One of the others slid on the slippery wooden surface that was coated in inner essence. Just as the woman gained her footing again, Alyssa came down full force on the top of her head with the heavy metal. The legit head-banger short-circuited her motor functions and left her diving into a seizure and looking like a fish out of water.

The previously driven third assailant's assault-ready angling stopped on a dime. She watched as a nefariously numb Alyssa beat her cohort's mental sphere like Ken Griffey Jr. swinging for the fences. She didn't stop until the exquisitely sculpted head was remodeled to resemble a raw extra runny hamburger-like texture.

In her stupor of pure panic, she accidentally dipped out of the field of play, violating the rules laid down by the evil architect of the event. Sebastian aimed his handgun accordingly and, without flinching, unloaded several shots that tore the poor babe's perfectly tanned back up.

It was an amplified acupuncture for the ages. One

that would give a sadist a hard-on; it did anything but heal. The Swiss-cheese of now unresponsive sinew dropped to the floor, quickly finding death before she even had time to hit the dead polished trees beneath her.

"Three minutes!" Sebastian screamed as if Alyssa hadn't been motivated enough already.

Sarah stared down from her elevated slim platform, a claret stream still exiting her food hole and a dark determination was drilled deep into her expression. She wasn't prepared to abandon her position yet. It had brought her safety through most of the event and she was ready to ride it out.

Sebastian turned to Jinx, "This should be good, these two always acted like best friends in the office, but it's one of those things where you just know they fucking hate each other. You know what I mean?"

The outlandish entertainer nodded slowly before returning a dead glare back to the girls.

Sarah had her heels flush against the wall as Alyssa pushed a chair closer toward her and stood up on it. She had no choice but to point her feet outward as the ledge didn't offer enough room to accommodate any other position.

When the first swing of the slugger landed, Sarah was able to kick her foot up and avoid the strike. Sarah was thankful for the inflexibly fixed paintings; she was clinging onto them for dear life. Alyssa's swing had cracked some of the wall and the tin reverberated against the narrow lip.

"Alyssa! What are you doing! You bitch!" Sarah bellowed.

The second swing came faster than Sarah could have anticipated, smashing into her dainty foot in a most torturous manner. The pretty painted big toenail cracked in a spiderweb fashion and the two beside it snapped sickeningly like the Macho Man's mouth mid-Slim-Jim commercial.

Her cries sounded deranged as the rose stem's thorn stabbed into her tongue, ripping the muscle as it did a dance of pain. Still, she was a badass; the thought of loosening her lockjaw-like bite never even crossed her mind.

While thoughts of losing never manifested, other things still did. The screeching hurt that rocked her exterior was impossible to ignore no matter what yoga DVD routines she tried to rehash. Sarah's focus had been fractured the same as her foot, and that's probably the reason her other leg didn't react when the bat pounded her opposite toes next.

The swipe shot upward, hyperextending the longest of her frail phalanges backwards. The heartless attack shattered her hallux and left it arching over toward her ankle. The double-dose of deformity had her looking like she was immersed in a Chinese foot binding fetish.

As Sarah's feet found a new outline, she fittingly lost her footing. With her balance beaten to a pulp, she plunged off the perch and landed hard on the ground below. It only took seconds for Sarah's "best friend" to pounce on her like a piranha to pepperoni.

She struck Sarah in the chest first. The tin twisted and splintered her sternum, causing an internal rupture immediately. The second hit dislodged ribs, clearing out and offering an unknown strike zone to her little racing heart.

"Let go of my flowers, you fucking cunt!" Alyssa shrieked in a tone that sounded fresh out of the asylum.

Sarah put one of her hands up toward her former friend as if trying to protect her face. She still hadn't relinquished her chomping grip from the scarlet and saliva-saturated stems, but the confidence that once sparkled in her sights had nearly vanished.

As the metal breast-beater came down again, Alyssa found herself smashing Sarah with the most catastrophic shot yet. In a sort of happy accident (for Alyssa), it landed in the slice of torso where the ribs had shifted. The vulnerable blood pumper felt the traumatic impact of the steel hit it so hard that it knocked it offbeat.

Sarah let a wheezing wind sweep away the accumulation of plasma that had been simmering in the rear of her throat. The spray of splatter speckled Alyssa but also made her smile. The stems had finally dislodged and fell to the floor beside her.

"One minute!" Sebastian screamed.

Alyssa dropped the bat and snatched the bloody tattered remnants of the nearly petal-less flower bouquet as Sarah performed her final expiring shakes. She was now timed to the bizarre new bumping rhythm of her internal ticker. But the song didn't last long—her fifteen minutes of fame were up.

Without hesitation, Alyssa dashed back toward a smirking Sebastian with the gory trinket. As the gap between her and her survival closed rapidly, nothing could stop her. Everyone was dead or too mangled to move. Everyone except for Nina…

Nina had been lying in wait, still under the table her mother had scrambled from minutes before. As she peered through the vanilla tablecloth, she saw

Alyssa come into frame. Alyssa's eager legs burned rubber a little too fast as she reached the dancefloor. And just like so many others, she stumbled and slid forward with the urgency of an MLB player stealing home.

However, unbeknownst to Alyssa, she may have popped the champagne a few seconds too soon. Her flashy finale was interrupted by the revenge-fueled, timid nineteen-year-old with a crushing death grip suffocating the butter knife in her hand. Nina was afraid, but she wanted to live. But maybe even more than life, she wanted retribution.

Relatively fresh out of high school, Nina was never an athlete, she was more of a sheepish nerd really. But being a geek was about to pay off. In biology class, Mr. Valentine had hammered home that if your jugular vein got shanked, it was pretty much a wrap for the injured.

The thought of the quirky teacher discussing his blue veiny diagram with a long metallic pointer remained in her head as she mustered every shred of force and propelled the dull blade into Alyssa's throat. Caught off guard, she'd somehow done it; Nina's practical target was penetrated by the cutlery that was just pointed enough to get the job done.

The neck flesh flapped as she twisted and popped the inner rosy roadways and let the juice flood out like a cherry mudslide. Nina felt Alyssa's body lose its tension and fall to the side. Finally, after what felt like an eternity, Nina felt her hands go limp and watched the soaked stems drop to the floor.

Nina was crying for many reasons. She looked to her left and watched the eruption of essence leave Alyssa as her legs shook wildly. Then, just a foot or two away laid her motionless mother. Olga's grave grimace and exposed brains were the last thing she'd hoped to see. Growing up Nina often wondered what went on inside her mother's head, but never had she hoped to see it that intimately.

Nina stared up glossy-eyed at Sebastian and then back down to the disgusting flowers. Did she even really want them?

"THREE!" Sebastian yelled at the pinnacle of his exuberance. "TWO!" Sebastian continued looking at Nina, highly interested in her actions and analyzing her decision.

Just before he howled out "ONE!" Nina snatched up the flowers and felt the prickle poke through her skin and the hot fluids from the other women enter her body.

"WELL, I'LL BE DAMNED! WE HAVE A WINNER! AND I'M PROUD TO SAY, WE'RE KEEPING IT IN THE FAMILY! EVERYONE, PLEASE GIVE A ROUND OF APPLAUSE FOR, MY COUSIN—"

Before the celebratory cheers could be offered, Olga, with her pinkish intellect partially exposed, launched herself upward. Nina's eyes lit up like a miracle had been unveiled before them. Knowing that the person she was closest to in life, the person that was always there for her, was still there (at least for a little while longer). The imagery of Nina's deformed mother was disturbing but still felt like it was the greatest gift of all. Until Nina saw what she was holding…

"What in God's name…" Sebastian mumbled, looking back to Jinx for counsel.

In Olga's left hand sat the elongated spiky heel

and the uneven severed foot that laid beside her on the floor. She quaked and shook like she was being manipulated by a malfunction. Like she'd been programmed to kill and was stuck on her last command regardless of who was in the crosshairs.

"Momma!" Nina cried as she drove the tip into her eye socket as easily as pushing a tac through a poster on the wall.

"What the fuck! You… th-the game ended! You can't—" Sebastian whined, losing his grasp on his next intended words.

Olga ignored Sebastian's remarks and forced her daughter onto her back. She then used all her weight to push down until the base of the heel was nestled against her brow. Clear and claret fluid meshed and the indent overflowed with a pulpy slop. Nina froze in place, losing her ability to move.

Olga snapped back around, flipping about, and scurrying to snatch up what was left of the stained flowers.

Sebastian looked at her and wondered if she had any comprehension of what she'd just done to her own daughter. *Did the head trauma send her off the deep end, or is it a clever ruse?* he wondered.

"Auntie! What on earth is wrong with you? Have you flipped your shit, or are you just a selfish hard-boiled cunt?" Sebastian asked.

She offered him no response—her brain wasn't in the kind of shape that allowed one to formulate even the most basic sentence. Olga just continued to shiver as she tried to hand him the flowers.

"NO! NO! NO! I'm afraid that won't do… You see, the game ended already, yet now the winner has been robbed of the spoils. The rules are the rules," he explained as he carefully elevated the handgun and aligned it with her ruined head.

"Unfortunately for you, Auntie Olga, killing your daughter, while highly entertaining, still doesn't make you a winner."

She would have pleaded if she had the capability to. But her mind mirrored the egg in the frying pan in the 'this is your brain on drugs' commercials.

His aunt's head had already been put through the wringer, but that didn't stop Sebastian from emptying the clip and turning a life-threatening deformity into a pair of shoulders with nothing left to hold up.

BOOGIE DOWN

The men had just finished separating from Cindy and Paula who still stood traumatized and gore-clad by the windows. The only remaining females in the room stared down Taylor with a wicked hatred — they knew that the events which had unfolded were random, but if Taylor wasn't such a societal tapeworm, her whack-job husband would have never sought after her. And as a result, they would not be in the helpless position that they all found themselves in.

Taylor didn't seem upset, she was emotionless. The bloody bride stood watching the men file out onto the dancefloor. A few had been enlisted previously to help Jinx clear the crumpled corpses, otherwise, it would have taken hours for the floor to allow enough space for what came next.

She'd watched the mysterious enigma take a lap around the dancefloor and dining area prior to cleanup. The jester surveyed each of the massacred bodies carefully. If they admitted the slightest semblance of life, Jinx made sure to extinguish it, complements of the AK-47.

For those that were already beyond repair, the odd entertainer's gloved hand slowly dragged them off to the side, or Jinx gestured to one of the men to remove them. The end result saw an enormous pile of ruin that looked holocaust-worthy.

When Taylor watched all of her friends be dragged away, it was like a little more pressure was lifted off her back. *Better them than me. But we are running out of them... I'm going to have to think of something soon... before there's no one left...*

As Perry worked his way through the mass of men in the dining area, he began to lift random, half-finished drinks off the nasty tables. Whether it was whiskey, vodka, or wine, it didn't matter. The men around him acted as a camouflage to his lush-like activities.

Keith looked at him, surprised by his forward actions, "How can you drink at a time like this?"

"How can you not?" Perry asked, dropping a vodka gimlet down with the quickness. "Something fuckin' wrong with you if you can do this shit straight, buddy." He grimaced and set the glass down only to pick up the next, "Ugh, goddamn vodka, how do people drink that shit?"

The mad rush and sheer volume and variety of drink combining in his gut had him feeling twisted. Perry could handle his Wild Turkey like swallowing water, but the uncommon mixture stewing inside of him was different. It was dealing him a feeling that usually took a hell of a lot more for him to achieve.

Being numb and shitfaced was the best he could hope for considering his position. He was a little happier now, a little looser, and maybe, most importantly, a little more confident. Traits that he had always aspired to project out into the world, but ones that had always been absent without the liquid courage constantly showering his gullet.

Ever since he was a young, awkward boy growing up on the rough side of the tracks, Perry had simply wanted to blend in. To not be judged by strangers. In bonding with the bottle, he had found his crutch. He felt the drink had allowed him that much in his life, but was it enough to save it?

"I'm not losing. You're not fucking losing…" Keith muttered under his breath, ignoring Perry's inquiry. He was trying to convince himself, but it was a hard sell. He wasn't at the office bullshitting a stakeholder on a conference call, he was bullshitting himself. A much more difficult task giving the situation they'd been facing.

"Baby boy, let me tell you something, and I hope it don't come down to it, but if it's between you and me, I ain't gonna be the one to give it up." Perry was now in the grips of the drink. He slurred his words slightly while allowing his self-assurance to spread its wings wide.

"I ain't the one, Mack. I ain't the one you wanna test, you understand me?" he let out a little laugh amid the pep talk, questioning no one in particular. Not for nothing, the new smashed glass version of Perry gave him a better chance at perseverance. Whatever the task was going to be, he felt ready.

"Alright, gentlemen!" Sebastian hollered as the men finished grouping into the freshly cleared out area. He held the AK-47 with a fresh clip loaded. "The ladies had their turn, now it's time to show them what we can do. But before we start, I need to ask a question. And let me stress, it's imperative that you all answer honestly."

While the flock of frightened males remained entranced by Sebastian's speech, Jinx subtly wheeled another rather obtuse box that was gift-wrapped over by the exit door. He began to methodically unwrap the paper from a seated position at the table some distance away. The jester was careful not to let anyone get a peek and spoil the surprise.

"DJ Buttaz, I'm counting on you for this one, brother, so be ready," Sebastian said.

The terrified DJ nodded obediently and smiled, but he was anything but thrilled to learn he was participating. *Just play that flavor, play those bangers, the surefire joints...* DJ Buttaz thought to himself, believing he could appease him.

"But to the larger group, I need you to follow my instructions right now. We all know, there are good dancers and there are bad dancers. It's just a fact of life. And right now, it's important that you ask yourself, which are you?"

"Let me remind you again to be truthful in your self-assessment. If I find out you're lying—and I will find out—you will find a far worse fate than you've seen previously on display. So, with that preface out in the open, I'd like all of you who believe you're shitty dancers to please congregate on the left side here," he said, pointing. "Up against the far wall there. Make room, judging by the looks of you, I'm sure there'll be plenty."

He then turned his attention back to the other direction, "And for those of you that think you've got the chops to cut up the rug, please assemble on my right side."

A nervous confusion took over the men, many of them had no idea. It wasn't the type of question they asked themselves regularly, if ever.

"C'mon, quickly now! You know if you suck or not, get moving!" Sebastian commanded.

Slowly, the humanity sifted itself into two-scale tipping disproportionate halves. All but several men found themselves in the shitty dance audience.

Perry stood next to Keith in the small group of men that had chosen to label themselves as the cream of the crop. He wasn't exactly sure what that meant or if it should give him a greater sense of survival security than the rest. The decision was made based on instinct and it was a good decision indeed.

When Jinx hoisted up the freshly unpackaged and fully-loaded AT4, the brigade of bad dancers were all still too focused on Sebastian's next words and command to realize what was happening. As the recoilless anti-tank weaponry launched the first rocket into flight, Jinx was already engrossed in the process of reloading the next before the initial missile exploded.

The violent blast took something from everyone and everything — including the building. The men's bodies came apart and painted the cavernous gap. The newly exposed and fractured underlying building materials were pelted with the warm innards of the various guests.

The magnitude of the explosion had been slightly miscalculated. As the room shook, the groom was launched backwards. The shrapnel flew; some hot glass shards and pieces atop the tables embedded into Sebastian's facial and shoulder tissue, tearing through his seven-thousand-dollar suit. He landed safely, still firmly gripping the machine gun in the pile of his dead in-laws.

The needle came off record and DJ Buttaz followed everyone else on the other side of the room as they landed hard on their asses.

"Son-of-a-bitch!" Sebastian barked, trying to regain his bearings and dig a big hunk of glass out of his skull.

When Sebastian opened his eyes, the blood in them made it seem like he was looking through rose-colored glasses. The many mangled men left an abominable imprint. The countless random limbs scattered about, the missing faces, and charred exterior created a melting pot of ghastly peril.

Somehow, amid the smoke and disorientation, a few stragglers hadn't become cut up enough to be part of the human butcher shop. One man was staggering around near the wall of the building screaming at the top of his lungs, "My eyes! I can't see! They took my fucking eyes!"

That they had, his state was no act. That much was displayed by the poor man's next step. Mere moment's ago, it would have been a step onto the floorboards that butted up against the wall, but now, it was into the thin air of the gaping hole that offered a new exit from the thirteenth floor of the Biltmore. He didn't get to enjoy the entirety of the fall, instead, he fell chest-first into the fraying rebar that was now sticking out in all directions. As his bones burst to allow space for the unforgiving metal to rupture its way through him, all of his gripes came to a sharp and absolute ending.

One man emerged from the smoke looking like a mangled extra in a zombie movie. He was eyeing Sebastian like he was about to jump on top of him, but the groom had enough of his senses to pull the trigger before he got close enough.

As Sebastian's burst of shells cracked against the aggressor's hips and pelvis, he dropped, bleeding in agony and unable to advance another inch. Out of the corner of his eye, he saw Jinx eyeing the remaining cluster of men and elevating the rocket launcher again.

The evil jester quickly found footing again, and as the second rocket let off, Sebastian dove toward the area where Perry, Taylor, DJ Buttaz, and the rest were all huddled.

This time, he was able to avoid the shrapnel but the strength of the blast assisted his airborne state like that predictable scene in every action movie where the hero is diving away from the explosion. As he sailed through the atmosphere, he touched down awkwardly.

The harsh landing caused the machine gun to rotate toward him. As Sebastian landed on top of the gun, his finger hyperextended and accidentally activated the trigger. A couple of shots let off and went ripping through part of his belly.

"Fuck!" he cried, feeling the deep burning sensation in his abs.

He glanced down at his gut and while it didn't

look good, he wasn't about to let it stop him. He had done away with most of them, there were only a few more left to accomplish his goal.

Sebastian quickly pushed the pain out of his mind and focused on the people before him. He couldn't let himself look weak in front of them. He sluggishly pulled the gun up and projected it in menacing fashion.

As he looked into Taylor's pupils just a few feet away, he knew there was a hidden happiness swirling inside them. A happiness for his hurt and pain. She wouldn't show it, she wasn't always that stupid. Especially when it would have most likely triggered immediate retaliation, but even though it was invisible, Sebastian knew it was there.

He wasn't quite ready to deal with her yet, they were still mid-contest. Sebastian looked back at the pure annihilation on the other side of the ballroom. The destruction looked like something out of a modern war film.

The bottomless hole that led to the chilly outside of the hotel and lack of life around it was astounding and beautiful. He took it in like inhaling a foreign cigar. But it wasn't quite stunning enough to leave him without fury.

Sebastian popped up off the floor and sprayed a burst of rounds at the ceiling. Then he looked over at Jinx and grabbed his bleeding stomach. His face and shoulder were also still torn up from the shrapnel, leaving him with a roughness hovering about him.

"Are you fucking stupid! You almost blew me to bits! I'm willing to die, but not fucking yet! You understand me!"

The creepy jester nodded and set the weaponry down on the table. Jinx then fished below for a moment. Seconds later, the wicked helper retrieved a handgun and promptly stuck the barrel to the temple of the oversized mask.

"No, no, no! I'm sorry! I didn't mean to yell at you... you're doing excellent. Please, we're so close now! It's me, it's not you, okay? Let's just finish this thing up. We're almost there, what do you say?"

Jinx registered Sebastian's plea and lowered the gun slowly. Then extended it back to the dwindled group of those who remained.

"That's the spirit," Sebastian smiled before applying more pressure with his arm against his bleeding gut. "Alright, the rest of the men get out here! Now! And, DJ Buttaz, man your goddamn station!" he yelled.

Perry, Keith, and three other gentlemen dragged themselves out to the still smokey dancefloor in reluctant fashion. The men looked up at him like a pack of dogs that were potentially about to be reprimanded.

"Alright, now that we have the amateurs out of the way, we can get down to the nitty-gritty. No one wants to watch some middle-aged fuckers that can't cut a rug anyway, am I right?"

A flurry of forced concurrence followed his query. They knew better than to disagree with him, they had been down that road before.

"So, here we are. Standing is the top of the class, the real men that can fuckin' boogie down. Well, you better not have been bullshitting me. I guess we're gonna find out pretty quickly anyway."

Sebastian continued clenching his bread basket

and pouted a moment before continuing. "You won't have to wait much longer; it'll all be done after a song. A song, I might add, that will be up to our very own floundering fuck boy, DJ Buttaz, to select."

Sebastian cranked his neck back toward the disc jockey, "So, you better make it a good one, slick."

As Sebastian returned his glare back to the participants, he noticed that one of the men had raised his hand. He looked at him, a bit annoyed, before nodding his head in a 'what the fuck do you want?' sort of gesture.

"I have a question…" he moused.

Sebastian unloaded several rounds of machine gun fire into his face, causing the man's cheek area to form a ruby pit and send his nose off toward the dining area. The man somersaulted backwards and out of the picture as particles of his head misted the surrounding air.

"And I've got an answer! Any other questions?" he screamed at the rest of them. "Good, because it's gonna be the same fucking answer. Now! When he starts the track, the five of you… pardon, the four of you will dance. You will give us everything you fucking have. And as you should, because as the song continues, whoever isn't maintaining the standard is gonna join quiz show back there."

Contrary to Keith and the other two men beside him, Perry was keeping loose. His vibe was as chill as a vacation. He moved his body around like a boxer might before a fight to get himself fired up and in the zone. This uncommon confidence that was circulating inside was a welcomed asset.

In a way, this was the moment he'd been waiting for all of his life. A moment to express his artistic side that had been suffocated since before the 70s. A moment to be included. *I ain't the one, I ain't going out like a punk this time,* he thought to himself.

"Holy shit, grandpa's ass is fired up. You guys better not sleep on him," Sebastian laughed.

The moment was something Perry never would have had the stomach to do if he wasn't being forced to. The grim circumstances were less than ideal but he still embraced it, even though the outcome was anything but certain.

Perry knew it would all come down to the song. In his heart, he knew he had skills, but he was a one-trick pony. Perry laser beamed at DJ Buttaz with a menacing glare. As if he could will him to select a jam you might hear kicking out of an oversized boombox on a stoop in Yonkers back in the day.

DJ Buttaz was formulating his own strategy as Sebastian tired of watching Perry warm-up and glared back at him in anticipation. *Three younger white boys, and one old black dude. At the end of the day, that crusty mother fucker is my best bet...* DJ Buttaz thought to himself selfishly.

He reached down into the milkcrate of records until he found it. He set the wax down and aligned it with the needle. The room waited in anticipation as the baby blue vinyl sticker started to swirl around. The print read: GRAND MASTER FLASH & THE FURIOUS FIVE. A little further below, the artist's name read: THE MESSAGE.

Perry could've broken down crying when he heard the thrashing of symbols and the trippy synth invade his ear canals. It wasn't just his style, IT WAS HIS SONG.

Each bar in the verses painted the portrait of the

life he'd lived. He had so many fond memories from afar watching kids break to the beat of the classic track that would undoubtedly live on forever. And while he'd never been comfortable enough in his own skin to join them, he'd practiced.

In his apartment building's vacant basement, Perry had set up a cardboard foundation. He'd laid it down gracefully on the cold floor and even put a few milk crates down there for seating (despite never finding an audience). During all of those hot summers in the 80s, all he did was practice in solitude. All he did was prepare for a day that never arrived. Until now…

"Aw shit!" Sebastian yelled. "I fucking love this song! I never thought you would've picked this! Let's see what you fuckers got!"

Perry's body was becoming possessed. During the buildup of the beat, his shoulders popped and his arms swam up and down as he screamed the words he'd been waiting to release since puberty. The question Grandmaster Flash posed to himself was one Perry had asked himself countless times during his upbringing. When shit got too real in his hood, and he was consumed with trying to keep his ass intact.

Sebastian's eyes lit up as he watched Perry's passions rip out from inside him. "Yes," he said under his breath, "this is what it's about!"

The other men looked lost, moving their arms, shaking their hips, and even snapping their fingers as they peeked at Perry for inspiration. But what the man was doing just wasn't in their wheelhouse.

As the sound of glass breaking blared out and echoed through the ballroom, Perry's old brittle pelvis cracked as he transitioned out of his top rock hype motions and dropped into a backslide. The blood-drenched floor helped him glide like a god as he twisted into a pair of back two steps. He then cycled into rotating between kickouts and crazy commandos. He was putting on a brilliant display of elderly athleticism for the ages.

As Perry immersed himself more in the dance, he screamed out the words and snapped back into his prehistoric routine. It was like he'd never stopped practicing, like he'd never left that dingy but cozy basement in Yonkers.

Perry belted out they rhymes, somehow able to spit the lyrics while continuing the flashy breakdance routine at the same time.

Each sentence he spat was reliving all of his impoverished experiences, every instant that he'd struggled to survive through. It was almost as if Grandmaster Flash had found him again to help aid in his survival. The words felt like so much more than just another dope song.

Sebastian was becoming so enthralled by Perry's epic performance that he shot the gun off at the heavens again. Then he looked at the others, who were anything but inspiring, and got a better idea.

"The old man is fucking killing you guys! Better get moving!" he yelled, shooting the machine gun at their feet like he'd seen in the movies.

But unlike the cliché comedies where the shots never seem to actually land, his were finding their mark. Keith was trying to keep up and doing his best impression of what he'd seen in the hip hop music videos. It was god-awful but slightly better than the rest. The men beside him weren't as quick with their feet, hence they weren't so lucky.

One had a slug tear the left half of his ankle open. The poor bastard plummeted to the dancefloor writhing in pain. Somehow, in ridiculous fashion, he was still trying to emulate the freshness that Perry was putting out. Bleeding, screaming, and dancing. Only at Sebastian's wedding day massacre could you see those three things at once.

The other fella beside him got tagged higher and multiple times. His injuries were more life-threatening so he wasn't trying to dance anymore. Instead, he was trying to stop the bleeding from exiting the dangling mix of bone and meat where his kneecap used to be.

The gruesome sight made Sebastian recall his own wound and how he was able to push past the pain. The deformed man seemed to enrage him. He lifted up the gun again and let a foul scowl manifest on his face.

"You're a fucking disgrace! The both of you!" Sebastian hissed before pulling the trigger again. The spray of bullets found their mark, sending a bloody spatter that touched both Keith and Perry.

But Perry was still in the fucking zone. He was already covered in blood from swirling around on the floor, the warm addition didn't affect him. His janitor jumpsuit was discolored and moist to the touch as he windmilled his way up off the slippery surface. Somehow, he was able to muster the upper body strength to keep himself poised to perfection.

Perry continued to maintain his lyrical output as he went back to the standing top rock moves for a moment. He was like a miracle manifesting as he continued the epic performance.

Keith continued to unveil his whack moves that felt like they were the culmination of a dad joke. While dripping buckets of perspiration, from the corner of his eye, he watched Perry knowing there wasn't much more time. When the custodian's old aching bones flipped into the monkey sweeps and then back to around the worlds he knew, he was fucked hard.

There was no way he was getting out alive. Keith's trajectory had taken a bizarre turn—he would be executed because he could not out dance a janitor. He almost wished he could've said it out loud before they killed him because it sounded so ridiculous. *When people think about the end of their life, they never think about that one... So, do I wanna get shot in the face? Not particularly... Maybe it's finally time to get my wings, but fuck it, I'll get them on my terms,* he thought to himself.

As Keith registered that the look on Sebastian's face had just switched to 'I've seen enough', he took off toward the massive hole that the rocket launcher had created in the side of the once regal ballroom. Jinx instinctively raised a handgun up at the fleeing contestant but Sebastian held the jester's arms.

"Let him go," Sebastian said.

Keith didn't hesitate; he looked like a gymnast the way he bounced off the cracked flooring and barreled through the enormous hole. He cleared the man that had been bayonetted by rebar a short time ago and was set to get the full effects of the fall.

He screamed inaudible moans on the way down and attempted to apologize for all of his sins on the way, but there simply wasn't enough time to seek forgiveness for everything.

Keith fell through all the darkness of the recently transitioned evening sky, knowing most likely that there would only be more darkness after it was over.

DJ Buttaz pulled the needle off the record just in time for everyone in the ballroom to listen to his body crash into the hood of an SUV. The annoying alarm was loud enough for them to hear faintly.

Sebastian looked at Perry who was panting like he'd just finished running a marathon and on the verge of regurgitation. A smile crept across his bloody face as he clenched his belly and continued to try and stop the bleeding. "Well, it looks like we have a winner," he said with a sinister laugh.

A NUMBERS GAME

"You knew we were gonna use it, but up until now, it just didn't make sense with so many people around," Sebastian explained to Cindy and Paula.

The duo still remained traumatized from all they'd endured, not to mention all they'd witnessed. While the blood on their bridesmaid dresses had time to dry up, they knew they were always only an unforeseen outburst away from getting soiled with a fresh coating again.

Sebastian caressed the side of the lethal chemical tank, wiping his bloody hand against the glass. The contrast of the green liquid and maroon warmth gave off a Christmas vibe you might expect to see in a serial killer's house.

"It's a numbers game now, I'm afraid. You see, Jinx and I aren't part of the calculation, but for the final celebration, I require balance. Right now, we have my man, Perry," he said, extending his hand for the high-five.

Perry quickly obliged him; it wasn't as if he had a choice…

"The talented DJ Buttaz," he said, turning toward him. "So, that's two men remaining… but then there's the three of you…"

Sebastian shuffled around in his pocket before finally extracting a nickel. "So, because my wife will, of course, need to be present until the end, being that it's her ceremony, that leaves you two," he flipped the coin and snatched it out of the air and slapped it down on the top of his hand.

"Unfortunately, it's time to trim the fat. Cindy, I always liked you best, so I'll let you call it."

Paula's face crinkled as she seemed offended by Sebastian's remark. Cindy began to perspire, considering all that was on the line with the fifty-fifty call she had to make.

She looked at Taylor who stood a short distance away. To Cindy, it was clear by Taylor's expression that she wasn't thinking about trying to reason with her twisted husband or making a plea for her closest friends. She was most likely consumed with figuring out her own next move. Cindy knew exactly how she operated—saving her own ass was the only priority in that self-centered brain of hers.

"Tails…" Cindy uttered as the choice coincided with the thought running around her head about Taylor's rump.

Sebastian removed his hand and peeked down at the uncovered coin. "Excellent choice, young lady!" he gleefully chirped.

"I'm sure you're wondering what all of this means, what the significance of a coin flip really amounts to. I think it's pretty obvious and easy to absorb. Anyone who's been to one of those traveling carnivals probably already knows."

He pointed up to the seat above the acid tank which was encompassed by a cage-like fencing. "Paula will take her seat here, and Cindy, because you won, you'll get the first three throws. Should you hit the target on any throw, your opponent will, of course, be dropped into this tank of nitric acid and other fun chemicals. I spent months perfecting this blend, it should dissolve one of you quicker than a tooth in a glass of Coke. Much quicker," he smirked.

Sebastian stuck his head over the small vat to look into the liquid. "As you can see, the phones that we dumped in here, what feels like ages ago, are no more. So, you can rest assured that once your tender flesh gets dunked, the meat should be sliding off bones like butter."

The girls were already crying before he could finish explaining what was about to happen. Paula turned to Cindy and gave her a hug, then pulled her mouth close to her ear.

"It's okay, I forgive you. I forgive you for everything. Just try to hit the target, don't think about it," Paula whispered.

"This is real fucking heartwarming, but just get in the goddamn dunk cage now, Paula!" Sebastian screamed, scooping up the AK from the table beside him and leveling it at her face.

As Sebastian watched her ascend the metal steps, he clinched his abdomen. It still burned from the bullet that had lodged itself inside his gut. He was having difficulty talking and focusing, but still, he powered through it. They were nearing the finish, there was no room left for weakness.

Jinx locked Paula in the cage after she slid inside, and Taylor's best friend carefully set her buttocks down on the narrow seat above the steaming acid. As the strong odor of the toxic chemical composition attacked her, she began to feel a bit woozy. Despite her lightheadedness, she tried to focus and control her breathing, but that was easier said than done.

"Alright, you see where that hand is?" Sebastian asked casually.

Cindy looked around a bit confused until her glossy eyes found a destroyed and blackened hand that was mangled severely from the rocket attack a short time ago.

"Yes, that one. That's the line. Don't step past it or the two of you will be trading places," Sebastian warned.

He reached over to the table where a baseball sat. It had been waiting since back when he had offered up his weathered but trusty Easton bat to the ladies. With everything else that was going on, the others had thought little of it. He tossed the white sphere with red laces toward her.

Cindy struggled to wrap her hands around the baseball before finally catching it. She ran her fingers over the threading, trying to comprehend what she was about to do. She'd already gnawed on a dead child's face, and while that action assisted in the countless murders of many staff, it wasn't actually her who had cut them to pieces. This was different. This was going to be all on her…

"You get three tries. Now, please, if you would,

proceed," Sebastian said, stepping away from the tank. He planned to avoid any splashing of the hazardous soup, clearly learning from the incident with the rocket launcher and nasty shrapnel.

The remaining survivors all followed his lead and created a safe distance from the dangerous drowning pool and their own carnal vehicles. All eyes were on Cindy as tears continued to secrete from her damp lids. She stared at her girlfriend, Paula, who gritted her teeth waiting.

The pause lingered like a broccoli and bean-based fart. A sense of dread and sadness clung to Cindy in addition to the fear of her own life being flushed down the toilet. If she missed, she might die, but if she landed the throw, she'd probably still die and then go to hell afterwards.

"Just do it, Cindy!" Paula yelled.

Cindy hauled back and dragged the baseball behind her ear and launched it forward. It felt like time stopped as the white leather rotated through the air. Still, it didn't take long to realize that the throw was completely off target.

The ball crashed onto the floor before it even reached the tank. It rolled to a standstill in the crimson that seemed to still dominate the majority of the spiffy ballroom floor.

Paula let out an exhale of relief and took in another deep breath of potent diabolic compounds emanating from the tank below. Her lungs burned as she tried to locate the current position of the ball.

"Christ, that was bowling shoe ugly," Sebastian snarked. He quickly scooped up the ruby orb and tossed it back to Cindy, who caught it with ease this time. "Do it again, but this time, do it like you understand that your ass is gonna be on that seat next if you fuck this up."

Cindy was feeling wobbly—the pressure of the situation couldn't have been more crushing. The target was massive and only about a mere car's length away in distance. Even her less than athletic delivery should be able to hit it without issue. In fact, she remembered being at a town fair some time ago and doing just that.

She envisioned everything she could remember from that dark evening. The glowing carny lights. The smell of buttery popcorn. The mustached man with the top hat and an urge to swindle in his eye. The sounds of the classic predictable circus-like music escaping cheap crackly speakers.

When Cindy cranked the ball back this time, she was more relaxed somehow. She even used a crow's grip around it as she again pulled it behind her ear. Maybe it was easier because she didn't see Paula and her grinding teeth and runny eyes. She didn't see the tortured and tormented wrinkles discombobulating her expression. Instead, she saw the silly clown in the striped outfit blowing on a whistle playfully. The same greasepaint-dipped smelly nomad who had already been dunked countless times that evening. Surely one more dip wouldn't hurt him, would it?

The pitch couldn't have been more accurate; it smacked the multi-layered target dead in the white dotted center. And when the stiff metallic ping resounded throughout the room, the seat shifted downward until it was completely vertical.

Paula screamed as gravity would become her doomsday, pulling her entire frame under the steaming poisonous concoction. Her insuppressible agony allowed a sizable swallow of the corrosive liquid to journey down her throat. The bubbling brew sizzled her digestive tract, leaving her intestines rumbling and her organs aching. While on the inside her critical cogs were painstakingly melting to mush, her exterior was in far worse shape.

When she resurfaced from the initial plunge into the bath of emerald-shaded syrup, her skin was cracking and raw. The once healthy cells were already beginning to break down. Paula's previously milky complexion was burning off and the blood and pigment was being forced to migrate south.

As her flesh dripped away from her body, the pain became unbearable. The dip had left Paula's eyes immediately scorched. Her mouth had sucked down plenty of acid, and her nose had pulled some of the destructive fluid deep into her sinuses. She coughed out in primal fashion while screaming at the top of her dissolving lungs. She felt around blindly, searching for some type of assistance that would never come.

The remaining guests looked on, horrified as the already disturbing devolved into something no one expects to see in their lifetime. The slimy sheets of her flapping skin peeled off as she scratched helplessly at her disgusting surface. They eventually slipped off altogether from her newly greased shell.

Paula gripped her bony exposed fingers around the cage's bars and elevated herself to a point where she was partially out of the now maroon mush pit.

"Don't even think about it," Sebastian remarked as he unloaded the hand cannon. He wrapped his arm around his throbbing gut and was pleased to see that the pain wasn't in vain.

The cluster of bullets found the mark without issue, causing a mini-explosion of gore and fingers to erupt. There was nothing left for Paula to hold on with anymore and she tumbled backward into the dreadful death pool.

Her screams were stunted again by a flood of the now amber liquid. She swallowed not only the noxious elements again, but also her own dissolving body tissue. She could feel the hairs running off of her scalp and her lips flattening and detaching from her mouth.

When she broke through the top of the liquid this time, she was far less vivacious. The only bubbliness about her was the seltzer-like fizz that accompanied Paula's gags and drool. Her fragmented fingers remained submerged as her body shut down.

She gurgled idly as any semblance of who she was dripped off of her face, exposing her creepy skeletal smile that had always been underneath. An expression that she'd never planned on showing the world had somehow found daylight.

CAKE

"And here we are again… the night has finally come to a close. Everyone seems to have had their fill," Sebastian said, surveying the slaughter that he and his wicked counterpart had left splattered all over the building.

He looked down at Perry, DJ Buttaz, Cindy, and his lovely wife who all sat traumatized at a small table that Jinx had just finished wheeling out. It had been obstructed by the gifts for the entirety of the evening and had a massive sign that read: DO NOT TOUCH!

The unhinged jester arranged a few of the gore-caked seats around the table with the mysterious veil draped over it. They could only imagine what was beneath it. The looming mystery pinched their insides like they were all filled with hungry insects.

"It's a sad thing really, I wish we never had to stop…" Sebastian coughed and spat up a mouthful of blood that dribbled down his shirt. "But like they say, all good things must come to an end. So, here we are, and somewhere within our group, there's a survivor. Someone left to tell the details of this otherwise unbelievable event. Someone who will be able to convey every bloody sadistic happening of my wedding day massacre…"

Sebastian approached Perry and placed both of his bloody hands on his shoulders. "Will it be you?" He continued on, next letting his drippy fingers move onto Cindy's shoulders.

"Each of you have made it this far for different reasons. Some of you are clever, some of you are resilient, some of you are selfish," he glared at Taylor who sat quiet and void of emotion.

"Maybe it's a combination. Maybe you just have a strong stomach, or maybe you're just incredibly frightened but are still able to follow basic directions no matter how horrifying. Either way, you're at the dance now, people, so fucking act like it. Act like you're ready to finish or I can just blow us all to kingdom come right now."

Sebastian extracted the detonator from his pocket again and fiddled with it carelessly. He was trying to get a rise from a group that was more stepped on than dogshit. They tried to humor his attempt with fearful, exhausted facials, but it all still seemed a bit forced.

"This last one you can all thank my lovely wife for…" Sebastian said.

More glares of discontent from the peanut gallery arose, targeting Taylor.

"Her and DJ Buttaz, that is…"

As Sebastian's hand came down on the disc jockey's flashy button-up and squeezed his shoulder, he jumped and let out a gasp.

"That's right, my sweetheart was out surfing the club scene, looking for ecstasy and the most sultry sausage, and our good friend here was all too happy to accommodate her. In fact, they even had a little lovechild together," Sebastian explained as he rounded the table to meet his terrified gaze.

"What the fuck?! Nah, man, you got it all wrong, bro, that isn't true! Taylor, tell 'em that shit ain't true," DJ Buttaz pleaded.

The others at the table would have been shocked by the revelation if they weren't already so broken down. They were as numb as a paraplegic's walking sticks.

Taylor sheepishly kept her head down. It was as if she knew something that the rest of the table didn't and had absolutely no desire to divulge it.

"Oh, he didn't know… not surprising, I suppose. There's a lot about my lady that people don't know." He turned his head from the DJ to his wife.

"But while you were out gallivanting and leaving a trail of stardust, I was watching. You probably forget, but the bills for those procedures end up on my credit card and you'd be surprised what you can find in the trash." Sebastian reached his hand into the center of the table.

"You'd also be surprised what you can find in the toilet for that matter too," he explained, jerking the curtain away.

He revealed a decent-sized wedding cake sitting all by its lonesome. One that was overall smaller than the lavish layers of sugary sweetness that sat across the room that they'd never gotten around to. But while it was maybe a quarter of the size, it did harbor some of the traits of their 'real' wedding cake.

For one, they were both splashed full of the revolting red human essence that made up their species. The difference being that the cake off in the distance had been pelted with hunks of carnal core after the many immoral episodes that they'd played out during the massacre. But the cake on the table was arranged much more deliberately.

The cake's white creamy circular outside looked like it had been decorated by Planned Parenthood. Sebastian had somehow managed to keep the fetus juicy even though it was months old. The beefy yet slightly shriveled unwanted embryo was slick to the touch. Its veiny trails and alien appearance came with a few other goodies.

Implanted around the ghastly almost-child was a disgusting fencing comprised of the extra-heavy flow tampons. They had over absorbed the mess that undoubtedly came after Taylor said 'good riddance' to the slimy seed. They were obviously just macabre décor as the already deathly docile flesh wad wasn't going to be moving or attempting to escape anytime soon.

The remainder of the perverse pastry was garnished with a variety of girthy blood clots that looked like some kind of bizarre dried-up jellyfish. In between the layers sat moist floppy slices of the amniotic sac. If all of the grotesque imagery wasn't enough, the bastard baby's tiny torso had been cracked open, exposing its minuscule organs like a fetal pig on dissection day.

Perry turned his head to the side and vomited. The chunky slush was comprised of mostly alcohol and burned on the way up. The old custodian's eyes watered and the stinging rancid fluid leaked out his nostrils.

"Sucker was nice and plump when I fetched him from the filter trap. I knew at that stage you'd be flushing the little bugger. You certainly waited long enough to deal with it, but then again, you always did tend to procrastinate, didn't you?"

The question was of a more rhetorical nature and Sebastian didn't really care to wait for an answer. As he eyed Jinx sliding the plates in front of the remaining guests, Sebastian took joy in the mortified frowns that manifested on their faces. They had done and seen just about everything under the sad sun, but this was beyond dreadful viewing, never mind the unsaid task that was coming.

"I think you all know what's about to happen next." Sebastian used the wide-bladed knife to cut down into the monstrosity. He made sure to distribute some of the various fetal parts, tiny organs, and other drippings equally onto each guest's dish.

"The rules are simple, the first to finish their plate wins the contest. I should specify though," he said, taking a seat beside and extending his arm around his battered bride.

"This contest will be a three-way dance. I have something extra special planned for my wife after this, but that doesn't mean she doesn't get some cake!" Sebastian scooped up a chunk of the under-developed tissues of his step-child and forced them into Taylor's mouth.

This would have been an acceptable practice at almost any other wedding. During most celebrations, the bride and groom always find their way into a food fight. She tried to resist but not too much. The butter cream-covered knife blade starting to split her neck open made it a vital choice to have a taste.

As the mishmash of the juicy dead cells spawned inside her slithered their way down her food canal, Taylor began to feel ill. Her body started to quiver but Sebastian alertly clamped his hand over her mouth, keeping her hatch sealed shut. With his other arm, he kept the sharp steel edge fixed to her throat until he felt her swallow it.

"Alright, now that my love has had her share, I think we can get started. My money's on Cindy, she's a fuckin' tank. The way she gnawed on that dead kid's face earlier… it just bodes well for her. What do you say, Jinx?" The creepy jester nodded robotically in agreement. Jinx let the AK-47 hang by the shoulder strap and removed an oversized meat tenderizing mallet from a small satchel that had been resting on the ground.

Sebastian stood up from the table and continued the trend of holding onto his bleeding abs with one hand while he cycled the bulky blade around manically in the other. Despite being wounded, he was every bit as intimidating as usual. He hadn't let his foot off the gas the entire evening.

Perry looked at the madness in his eyes and knew nothing would change it. He shifted to DJ Buttaz and then back at Cindy who both also seemed to understand that whatever words they said would only bring them closer to being dead. It was time for action, immoral, perverse, vile, disgusting action.

Perry sucked the remaining pieces of acidic barf out from between his teeth and spat them on the floor below him. He knew that this bout would be a quick one. There was only so much of the deceased fetus to go around. The cake portion that the abortion had bled into might be the most difficult part to get down.

Part of the head, and arm… Ugh, don't throw up again or you're dead. Is it too big to swallow in one shot? I'm gonna have to chew it, I think. Cindy is already familiar with this type of task… there'll be no room for hesitation. One fail, keep your eyes on her, she's the one to watch out for. DJ ain't got the heart for this. I can see it in his eyes…

Perry tried to find the motivation to move forward but he struggled. It felt like time had slowed while Sebastian stalked his way around the table. Then, suddenly, it hit him. Just like in the dance contest, he had already lived the answer.

In a medium that felt almost spiritual, Perry flew out of his current situation and back in time; way back. To the point of reference where his memory was foggy. He had no way to validate if the vision was a conjured fantasy or a subliminally suppressed recollection. But everything he felt and his eventual outcome all seemed to point toward legitimacy.

Suddenly, he was a baby in his mother's arms. He felt a rough scratchiness against his new delicate skin of the irritating scabs that riddled his mother's extremities. The ones that oozed with blood and pus while constantly trying to regenerate. They were the various holes that she stabbed into looking for a quick fix to escape the filthy world that surrounded her. To escape the responsibility that Perry had pushed into her. Momma's diet of drug use and sexual promiscuity was all she lived for. She wasn't fit to live for anything else.

She sat in the grimy rocking chair shirtless. Her ribcage was overly defined and her breasts had shriveled and become void of the nurturing essential succulence that his newborn body ached for. The polluted areola left much to desire.

When she inserted her nipple into his toothless mouth and he suckled, no nourishment was provided to him. Instead, a black used motor oil-like substance began to dribble out. The toxic teat gave him no joy as he screamed and cried in revulsion.

He leaped forward in the timeline from there. Back to the late nights without sleep in Yonkers. Back to the deep stabbing hunger pains piercing his guts relentlessly. The empty cupboard that his momma was always too absent to ever fetch food from. The one he opened in disappointment day after day. The one that had the dead rat rotting inside it.

His belly hurt so much that, in his mind, he never had a choice in the matter. When there was nothing left for him, and the people outside were too scary to ask for help, he was left to decide. His unseasoned mind had very little leverage in making his assessment. He had no guidance and, therefore, his primal instincts took hold of him.

He chose to sink his teeth into the gamey putrid pest. There was simply nothing else available to accommodate his hunger. And while the maggots tasted mushy and bitter and animal bones snapping between his baby teeth sounded like nails on a chalkboard, eating the foul carcass helped stop the pain. As the hairs tickled his throat and the decaying hunk landed in his pit, he felt better than before.

"GO!" Sebastian screamed, interrupting Perry's nasty flashback.

As Jinx stood between Perry and Cindy watching ominously, Sebastian got directly behind DJ Buttaz.

The sudden interruption didn't matter to Perry. He didn't have anything left to think about. If his constant adolescent hunger spells had taught him one thing, it was to be grateful. If he ate that fucking rat, that meant he could damn well eat that fucking baby too.

His hands shot down to his plate before anyone else's could've hoped to. He popped all of the baby parts and a watery blood clot into his mouth and ground the petite meat down without issue. Perry wasn't even focused on the rest of them, he was focused on trying not to starve.

After a few chews, he'd already swallowed. DJ Buttaz and Cindy were still trying to mash their mouthfuls and had failed to get all of their fetal parts on the initial swoop. All that stood between Perry and walking away from the hell he was in was one extra-large blood clot and a handful of cake.

He kept his pace and shoveled it in without the slightest hesitation. As he mashed it down into a fine puree, the others were just getting their final bites into their mouths. But as his competition began to chew, Perry had already swallowed. He unhinged his jaw and stuck his tongue out for Sebastian and Jinx to inspect.

Jinx acted first, driving the spiky mallet down into the back of Cindy's skull. The sickening crack sent the fetal parts and cake shooting out of her mouth and drove her forehead into the tabletop. The blood leaked out in all directions as the triangular metal tips rained down again, shattering the back and making contact with the cortex.

While Jinx was busy beating Cindy's brains in, Sebastian had grabbed a handful of DJ Buttaz's locks and started sawing back and forth over the front of his throat. His arms flailed about but he seemed content in giving up. It appeared as though, after all the bullshit he'd been through, he was now ready to embrace his death like he'd been waiting for it.

Sebastian had caught him mid-swallow which made for a particularly gruesome decapitation. Just as he was pulling the party boy's head off his shoulders, the pieces of the baby that he'd tried to force down were being reborn out of the hole where his throat had been.

Taylor and Perry both remained as still as trees in a dead wind while they watched the pair of psychos finish their business. They didn't know what to expect but at least they'd made it to the end.

Sebastian held up DJ Buttaz's still twitching face and gawked at it. Then he slowly walked over to the hole in the side of the building and tossed the head through. It dropped down the side of the building, and as he watched it descend rapidly, he hoped the DJ could still register what was happening during the massive fall.

When Sebastian turned back to observe Jinx, the nefarious jester appeared to be stuck in autopilot; hammering the pile of pieces that had previously comprised Cindy's pretty little head.

Sebastian smiled, grabbed his stomach again, and winked at Jinx. "It's time."

FAMILY PORTRAIT

Sebastian watched Jinx finish dragging the park-style bench over to the center of the ballroom. The jester looked back toward him as if awaiting further direction.

"Keep going, over a little more. Almost, just a little bit further, yep. Right there, perfect!" he replied in ecstatic fashion.

Taylor and Perry stood a few yards away looking at the disturbed groom as he got ready to bring the evening to a close. He used some of the blood still leaking out of his head to slick back his hair.

Perry was waiting patiently, trusting that the deeds he'd performed to appease Sebastian were enough to help him escape with his life. After all, he seemed quite hellbent on ensuring that there was someone left behind to immortalize him.

Taylor was the polar opposite of the aged janitor standing beside her. She was rattled to the core and felt death was just around the corner. She knew Sebastian had saved the best for last. Whatever he had in store for her would most likely be tenfold worse than anything she'd seen to that point. She still had a chance, but time was quickly running out.

Sebastian turned and stepped over toward the cake table where Perry and Taylor nervously waited. "Honey, would you please go and take a seat on the bench? Jinx is going to take our wedding photo now. I just need to have a brief word with the old man here first."

She remained silent, mind racing nonstop, but as usual, she obeyed his commands. Once she'd left them, Sebastian turned back to him. Then he looked down at the gross tabletop. He toyed playfully with the handle of the tenderizing mallet that was still stuck in the brainstem of Cindy's head.

"Listen... um... sorry, actually amid all the craziness, I don't think I ever caught your name—"

"Perry!" he interjected. "Perry Jackson, mister, Sebastian. And, sir, I promise you, I'm gonna make sure everyone knows every goddamn event that happened here today. I'll make sure they remember you, I won't let 'em forget," the old man promised.

"You know, out of everyone, I liked you the best, Perry. That was a hell of a ride, wasn't it?"

"Yes, sir..."

"But the thing is, Perry, I never planned to make it out of here. I was always gonna go down with the ship. But that whole 'maybe you'll walk away routine' was just... it was just me dangling a carrot," he said, picking up the mallet along with some of the

221

squished brain matter.

Perry's hope crashed to rock bottom—he got a feeling deep in his stomach that was different than anything he'd felt in his life. It was the hand of death massaging him.

"I'm sorry, old-timer, but I've already got Jinx to tell the story for me," he explained, suddenly driving the sharp part of the tool into his grayed hairline.

The severity of the swipe let a resounding thud echo through the ballroom and landed so deep that it ripped away a crooked patch of his skin.

The old custodian's eyes rolled up into his head as he dropped to the floor like a sack of garbage. Sebastian then extracted the handgun from his suit pocket and aimed it square at his chest and pulled the trigger like it was just another day at the office. The speedy bullet blew through his blood-saturated maintenance uniform and caused his body to jolt.

"If only I could stick around a little longer, your grave would have been one that I would've enjoyed dancing on." Sebastian collected the blood and snot from the back of his throat and spat the wad on Perry's face before he headed for his bride.

Sebastian spun around and caught a glimpse of Taylor sitting precisely where he'd told her to. She looked incredibly concerned, which was why an evil smirk was tightly spread over his lips.

"Alright, my love. I hope your special day was everything that you dreamed of. It will certainly be unforgettable, I don't think there's any disputing that…"

He slid into the seat beside her, "But before we say goodbye, we need to take our photos. JINX!

How do we look?"

The jester stuck a gloved thumb up in their direction and nodded the scary mask slowly.

Sebastian's grin had morphed into a grimace as he applied pressure to the bullet hole in his side. His hair was sweaty and wet with blood. The shards of glass from the explosion had left him torn up to a point where he projected an almost zombie-like look. The only constant since his initial speech was the manic expression that dominated him.

Taylor wasn't in much better shape. Her hands were still punctured and bleeding from the rose bouquet that Sebastian had pushed into her skin. Not to mention the lengthy deep lacerations on her shoulder from when he'd carved into her with the knife blade.

She glanced down defeatedly at her destroyed dress, trying to block out the throbbing pain of her seared tongue. The scratchy overcooked flesh felt rough against her gums. She couldn't have been less prepared to take a photograph.

Jinx had located an old Polaroid camera from the many evil gifts. It seemed like they could pull almost anything from there. The jester set his dead gaze upon the two of them and readied the camera.

"Say cheese!" Sebastian yelled, revealing his red-stained teeth for the photo.

The flash went off, and out of the corner of his eye, he could see that Taylor hadn't smiled for the picture. "I said say fucking cheese, goddamn you! Now, take it again, Jinx!"

Taylor forced a leer of pure agony just in time as he snapped the second picture. The Polaroid spat out of the front of the camera and dropped down onto the blood-littered floor below.

Sebastian stood up from the bench and looked down at his bride, "Follow me, dear."

"Sebastian?" his name sounded funny now when she pronounced it with her muscle subtracted tongue.

"Yes, love?"

"May I ask one favor of you?"

He nodded his head more out of morbid curiosity than anything.

"Before whatever comes next… would you allow me one more picture?"

"But, darling, we've already taken two and I think you did a splendid job on the second snap. Wouldn't you say?" he asked, looking to Jinx for confirmation.

The jester nodded gravely.

"You know I'll do whatever you want, darling, but if I could just have one more moment with my family. One last picture of us all together, it would mean the world to me," she pleaded politely.

Her husband pondered the ask. After a moment, his wickedly joyous expression grew a little further. He clasped both of his palms together and squeezed. "I think that's a fabulous idea. That is one fucking picture that I've got to see," he laughed, coughing up another collection of blood-conquered saliva.

"But, baby, I'm not feeling so hot. Would you mind helping Jinx drag them over here?"

"Of course, you're the one doing me the favor…" she replied.

Taylor got up as Jinx immediately began to walk toward the stack of her deceased family members piled by the stage. The jester was walking with a purpose, there was no way that she would be able to get there before him.

Jinx approached the mushed mask of gore that was formally Taylor's mother's face, the decapitated corpse of her brother, and the bullet-riddled body of her father. It appeared the creep was deciding who to take first before finally wrapping his finger around the wrists of Taylor's mother.

She exhaled a sigh of relief, and as Jinx began to drag her mother away, Taylor quickly latched onto her father. He was pretty heavy but she was highly motivated. The blood helped him glide across the floor but also made the footing more treacherous.

Don't fall over… Keep it up… Just get him to the fucking bench. Only a few more feet away, she rambled on to herself, curling her toenails into the wet floor for any extra grip she could manage.

Jinx had already left her mother propped up on the left side of the lengthy seating and was returning back for her brother. As Taylor lifted her father up, she could see his deflated lung partially peeking out of the gaping void in his backside. She continued to muscle his body onto the other side, being careful to leave a space beside him.

She plopped down on the bench beside his garbled carcass and her wrecked mother. Just as she was settling in, Jinx was returning with Christopher… well, part of him. Jinx tossed his decapitated head down on the floor in front of the three of them. The jester must have been tired of lugging around corpses so, apparently, that would have to suffice.

Sebastian was getting weaker by the moment, hoisting up the camera had even become more of a challenge than initially anticipated.

Jinx rejoined Sebastian and the two stood just far enough away to get all of Taylor and the members of her dead family in frame for their final picture together. Sebastian grinned as he watched more tears trace over the previous columns of moist make-up that ran down her beautiful face.

Sebastian tried to steady the camera in his shaking hands. "Don't ever say I didn't do anything for you. This married life, it ain't too bad is it?"

Taylor eyeballed Jinx who stood highly relaxed, hands at each side of the uniform, waiting for Sebastian to snap the photo. It was now or never.

As the camera flashed, her bloody hand snaked into her father's inside pocket and she extracted the revolver flawlessly. By the time Jinx saw the chrome glimmer of the gun's exterior and got the AK-47 in hand, a slug had already left the chamber and crushed into the sternum of the sinister bastard.

As the jester levitated backward, Taylor pulled the hammer back and sent a second wad of streaking lead just a couple of inches to the side of the first. The impactful violence sent Jinx crashing hard onto the dancefloor. Then, without hesitation, Taylor turned the hand cannon to her husband.

Sebastian was taken aback and let the camera slip out of his hands as it shot out the disturbing picture. It dropped in what felt like slow motion to the wet ground and broke into two pieces.

"Baby, please, we can work this out!" he pleaded.

"I don't think so," she replied.

"Yes, yes, we can! Just tell me what you want, what is it that you want?!"

"I want a divorce."

Those times when Dad had taken her out to fire a few shots at bottles on a fence came in handy. When she pulled the trigger, for the first time all night, her hands were steady. In a way, it almost felt like Anthony himself was exacting revenge as the shot left the barrel and made a savage entry into the maniac groom's throat.

Sebastian fell to the ground, twitching and the choking noises bursting out of the juicy wound where his Adam's apple used to be housed only intensified. He clasped both of his hands around his neck in an effort to hold what was left of it together.

"You sick fuck! You ruined my wedding day!" she screamed, unloading what remained of the bullets into his dying body.

She continued to pull the trigger mindlessly, well after the cylinder had been spent. The faint clicking noise resounded over and over like a broken record. Maybe it was fitting because now and forever she would be a broken person. The mental damages having taken their toll, a trippy feeling took hold of her. Taylor felt like she was anywhere but reality.

She looked around at the ballroom trying to take in the sum of collective horrors that surrounded her. The body parts, the demolished humans, the bodily fluid, the destructive weaponry, and the incredibly disturbing nature of the event that was supposed to usher her into social stardom.

Her face turned red and she dropped the empty gun. As it fell beside her stained feet, she started to cry again. Not because she had found a way to survive. Not because her poor family and friends were slaughtered with a hellish methodology. None of that seemed to matter to her.

She looked at the enormous pile of dead bodies in the corner near the hole in the Biltmore's exterior. Then down at the river of blood on the floorboards.

"Ughhhhhhh! My fucking phone is melted!" she screamed, recalling that her deranged husband had dissolved all the communication devices.

Until that moment, part of her had realized that although her wedding was ruined, there still might be a way to capitalize on it. She could have captured some exclusive footage of the aftermath of the massacre and made a killing off of it. Or maybe even posted it on her page.

"Goddamn it! Probably couldn't have put it on Instagram anyway, they'd just fucking censor it!" she moaned.

Suddenly, the bathroom door burst open, startling Taylor. She ducked down for cover near the bench behind her mutilated family. Then, she realized who it was.

"Taylor, I'm coming, baby!" Lucas yelled.

"Lucas?!"

"Yes, baby, it's me, that fucking psychopath didn't hurt you, did he?! Are you alright, baby doll?"

"He hurt me real bad," she managed to say in the clutches of sadness.

Lucas rushed up to Taylor and wrapped his arms around her bloody body, nestling her close. He moved in and kissed her on the lips. He wanted to show her that her deformities didn't bother him in the slightest. No matter how many slice wounds or stab punctures riddled her, he still had a thing for the girl. But he didn't expect what he felt next.

The slimy kiss tasted of blood and crisp flesh. The

crudely soldered tip of her tongue was rougher than a sidewalk. He pulled away from her and a bloody string of saliva stretched, still connecting their mouths momentarily. He then used the arm of his suit to wipe the red dribble from his lips. He had been wondering why her annunciation sounded a little strange…

"Well, looks like he can't lift a finger now…" Lucas said happily.

"No thanks to you!" Taylor snarked.

"What did you expect I do? That I should just stroll on out here and get massacred like the rest of these fools? I was waiting for the right moment."

"If you waited any longer, I wouldn't have had another moment!"

"Nonsense, I knew you would find a way to outsmart them. That's what attracted me to you in the first place… your incredible intelligence," he lied but his true motive was just a sentence away.

"This is so fucking dumb! How could this happen to me? What did I do to deserve this?!" Taylor whined, stomping her heels.

"You didn't do anything, baby. It wasn't you, the best thing you can do is just forget about this fucking abortion of a wedding. Put it in the rearview, okay? You know why?"

"Why?"

"Because I'm gonna give you a wedding that is tits above anything that's ever been done before."

A twinkle of happiness appeared in her reddened pupils. Much had been carved into and off of her body, but her mind was where the most pain was. The uncertainty was already creeping up. The screeching thoughts of insecurity began to worm their way inside her brain.

She no longer had a lock on being the prettiest girl in the room anymore. Kissing would clearly never be the same again with her toasted tongue. The plastic surgeons could probably do a lot, but something told her that tongue tips weren't in their toolbox.

When Lucas made his move, it was smooth as silk and well placed. He was more than familiar with how to capture a female's interest when she was feeling vulnerable. Just like every single time before, it worked like a charm.

"Oh, Lucas, I love you," Taylor cooed, wrapping her arms back around him again.

"I love you too, babe. And on the plus side, since Sebastian's fuckin' dead now, we get all the money!"

"Wait, what do you mean we?"

Just as the question of greed finished leaving her lips, the familiar sound of machine gun fire erupted. Both Taylor and Lucas winced in fear, but even as the shooting continued, none of the dozens of bullets seemed to find their bodies.

When they finally had the courage to look toward the direction of the gunfire, they saw Jinx in the sit-up position aiming the AK-47 high above both of their heads. Before they had enough time to look up, the massive, gaudy chandelier had come crashing down on top of them.

The weight of the angled lighting landed square on Taylor's head and folded her over sideways. The impact altered her outline in a manner that the skeletal system simply couldn't accommodate. Along with the shattering of glass came the splintering of bones.

Taylor's crumpled frame laid disproportionately mangled. One arm twisted in the wrong direction like a broken Barbie and the other snapped clean in half. Her mashed face looked like a mop that had absorbed an inordinate amount of blood.

The compound fracture piercing through her skin was a Faces of Death special. She would no longer have to worry about the societal stigma around the distortions that her body had suffered from any longer. It was a short-lived conundrum.

Her lights went out instantly and she was robbed of the stardom that she had always dreamed about only to be shuffled into an infamy that she never could've imagined.

When the shooting started, Lucas, always the coward, had taken a step back. That step was just enough to allow him survival. He wasn't crushed by the falling fixture but, instead, sent reeling.

As he bumped into a destroyed table, Jinx took aim at him again, keying in on the head. He let a burst of shots ring out that tore through his brain matter and sent fat lumps of his sneaky intellect spraying out behind him.

As Jinx heard Lucas hit the floor, the machine gun finally dropped. There was no one left to kill. The mysterious and murderous jester suddenly had no direction. The gloved hands pinched the bulky mask at each end and separated it from the creepy costume.

Dorian's expression was set to hurt. The pain seemed quite severe, but it wasn't of a physical nature. The sturdy Teflon vest beneath his outfit had seen to that. It was for the man that was just as wicked as he was. The man who paralleled his own perversion. It was for the man that he loved.

He quickly rushed over to Sebastian and fell to the ground in a dramatic fashion. However, it was too late, his infatuation had already expired. That didn't seem to matter to Dorian, though.

The disturbed wedding planner put his thin lips against Sebastian's, and as the reservoir of nasty red remained slowly drizzling from his mouth and throat, Dorian laid a porno-worthy kiss on him.

He cried for his client as he slurped away and grabbed at the corners of his collar passionately. He had become so much more than just another job. During their preparation, he'd fallen head over heels for the sexy businessman. He didn't mind that he was a little fat, he made up for it below the belt. Besides, his thoughts and ambitions were far more important stimuli for him to enjoy.

Once he finished his brief and romantic farewell, Dorian walked over to Lucas's fresh corpse. He removed his jester outfit and the bulletproof vest in its entirety. Next, he stripped Lucas down and slid the clothing that comprised the costume he was previously wearing onto the dead businessman's body. It didn't fit perfectly, but it would do the trick.

"It's time to smear someone's reputation," he snickered, still letting a few tears leave his eyelids.

Dorian finished strapping on the flak-jacket and adjusting the rest of the attire he'd worn while he slaughtered everyone. He raced across the room and retrieved the empty AT4 rocket launcher and put it into Lucas's still warm hands. And just like that, Lucas was the culprit behind the massacre.

"Can't believe it, he even worked with him, it's a perfect conspiracy," Dorian thought aloud.

Just as Dorian had about made his way to the exit, suddenly, he stopped. He turned back around like a lightbulb had suddenly gone off inside his head. The wedding planner ran back over to the bloody pool where Sebastian's corpse laid and looked down.

The picture of the beat-down bride and groom was a classic. They had been through a war. They had been through hell. Their horrific disfigurements shined as proudly as their perverted smiles. It was the second one, after Sebastian yelled at Taylor and forced her to grin.

"It's a masterpiece," Dorian whispered, bending over to pick it up. Once he had the messy photo between his fingertips, he headed for the exit and never looked back.

***

Dorian walked deep enough into the forest to finally locate his car. He preferred to be safe than sorry, so with caution in mind, he had left it in a remote area of the woods that was about half a mile away from the Biltmore.

Although the area was dead as far as traffic was concerned, and the hotel wasn't in use outside of the wedding they'd planned, there could have certainly been a straggler or two who dropped by. That was just a risk he'd come to accept.

He plopped down into the SUV, exhausted as always. Then he pulled out a black square book that sat under the passenger seat and laid it on top of the cushion. When the cover peeled back and he flipped through the pages, a spread that contained a handful of other nightmares was put on display.

Each picture was unique but also the same. The morbid collection displayed numerous brides and grooms who were all beaten to a gory pulp and torn apart. They were all in the same sickening spirit as the bloodstained photo that he was readying himself to insert and act as his newest addition.

As each of their haunting smiles stared back at him, he couldn't help but be aroused. Every time they looked his way, he recalled the fond memories of the wedding day massacres that he'd performed for each of his clients.

Sebastian would always be the cutest one of them all, though, because he thought he was making history. Little did he know, for Dorian, the grand form of slaughter was becoming old hat.

CLOCKING OUT

When his lights came back on, the room was quiet and still. Perry's eyes peeled apart slowly, the right one took some additional effort. The dried plasma that had finally quit flowing from his forehead had congealed. The old man had to push the coarse and crusty crimson away before his full vision was reallocated back to him.

Perry's breastbone ached where the hot bullet had launched into him in addition to his throttled noggin. The stiff blow from the tenderizer had most certainly concussed him, and the drowsy hangover from the collection of drink types he'd swallowed only amplified his state of stupor.

Perry didn't really know how long he'd been out for or why exactly his chest area throbbed in pain; everything went black before Sebastian had fired the shot. The shot which Sebastian had believed to have pierced through Perry's blood pumper.

After a few minutes of staring at the ceiling and wondering, he was finally able to sit up. He pressed his hands to his body and felt a solid object beneath the bullet hole in his frontside. Perry unzipped his suit pocket and slipped his wrinkled hand inside.

He pulled out his trusty companion, and to his utter amazement, a single bullet sat firmly wedged halfway through the steel flask. The drink had a body count that was on par with cancer. Most people that built it ritualistically into their regimen or used it as a crutch ended up wrecking their car or ruining their lives. But in Perry's odd circumstance, it had actually saved him.

He looked over at the fallen chandelier and Taylor's brokenness. He saw Jinx's unmasked but pulverized head. He didn't expect to know who he was, he wasn't connected to any of the people in the room, but a part of him wanted to see what the monster under the mask looked like.

It was something he might never be able to know now for reasons he was unaware of. Even when the police and media finally identified him, the real culprit behind the horrors that Sebastian's helper had committed was already far away from the violent scene.

Knowing he couldn't account for any of his curiosities, he scanned further, searching through the carnage for the man of the hour. He knew he couldn't be safe until he located that sick man's body. Finally, Perry spied Sebastian's bullet-riddled cadaver and let a conclusive wave of relief wash over him—he was alone now, thank God.

As Perry gawked down at the now crumpled steel flask in hand, his internal reflection was quite profound. While the evening of traumatic terror had undoubtedly scarred,

and in a sense validated his life-long reclusive mindset, there were still some things he'd learned. Demons that he'd exorcised which had been haunting him for the duration of his existence. For that, he felt a very strange sense of gratitude.

The situation had made him feel like he was trapped inside of a pressure cooker, but when shit hit the fan, he delivered. While everyone who had witnessed his gusto and performance would be too dead to tell the tale, that didn't matter. Getting credit was never something that mattered to him. Just knowing that he'd done it himself was all he needed for his peace of mind.

Sure, the whiskey had saved his life. If he hadn't been an alcoholic, he might never have survived the ordeal. But if he hadn't been a drunk, he most likely wouldn't have been buffing floors for a living either. He most likely would never have made his way into the brutality that transpired on the 13th floor of the Biltmore. Was it all part of a greater plan? There was no way to know for sure, but in his mind, it was a sign. He'd been given another chance.

Perry tossed the tin container that had got him through so many dark times onto the floor beside him. Suddenly, he knew with a profound certainty which had never come close to dawning on him before, that things were going to change. In his heart, he knew that the ringing hangover that pulsated a pounding pain in his tired brain would be the last one he ever experienced.

He decided in that moment that he was done feeling sorry for himself. Surviving the ordeal had instilled him with a loud and unignorable sense of appreciation. Maybe being married wasn't all it was cracked up to be. Maybe he had it all wrong and the envy he'd initially felt for the deceased duo was misplaced. It just took him a wedding day massacre to realize exactly how lucky he'd been all along.

Perry took one last look around at the hundreds of dead bodies, bits and pieces, and overall barbarity of the ballroom before shifting his focus to the exit door. It had been left unshackled and was calling to him.

"I ain't cleaning this mess up," Perry muttered, pulling himself to his feet.

FIVE STARS

Dorian sat in front of the massive monitor of his hulking desktop. Parts of the room looked closer to a spaceship than an office. The hardware bordered on obsessive, but to him, it was really just about business. He needed to be a phantom in the perverse universe of the dark web that he was dwelling.

The security was a necessity if he was to continue to offer his twisted services to the top-tier creeps around the globe. Business had been good the last few years. He was in a bit of a niche market, there weren't too many wedding planners that could work mass murder into the equation. So, when he found a potential client that was actually deranged enough to even think that notion was a possibility, he kind of had them by the balls. It wasn't exactly something a quick Google search could take care of.

Sebastian had been his first client to hold their wedding in America. Also, the first client he'd had relations with, which made the sure bet suicidal finale that his customers always worked in more difficult to cope with. Sebastian didn't end up committing suicide, but he achieved the result he wanted. One-hundred percent casualty rate (as far as Dorian knew). So, in the end, Dorian believed he'd delivered on every parameter that he desired.

Dorian had felt a little weird about arranging a massacre in the country he lived in. America was highly monitored and the chance of getting caught was far higher than any of the other shithole destinations he'd arranged for past clients. But he just loved Sebastian so much that it completely blinded him. Deep down, he'd wanted both of them to escape together in the end. He thought he could convince him, but Taylor snatched that opportunity away from his well-manicured fingers.

With his love probably sitting on a cold autopsy table somewhere, he looked to the perversion of the internet's seedy underbelly—the dark web—for his escape. Currently, his computer screen was occupied by a large group of adolescent children dressed as pilgrim skeletons. They were tearing apart a pair of middle-aged white folks.

The terrified man and screaming woman who, to the more sensitive public, were clearly culturally appropriating by being dressed in Native American garb, were finally dead. Although, they'd probably be killed again by internet trolls in the near future…

"The Best New Kids? Yeesh, this is fucked up," Dorian whispered to himself. "Alright, time to check out the reviews…"

He'd been waiting a little while to check them because of how sentimental thinking about that evening and Sebastian had been. In his business, the reviews got put up in advance because there would be no way for them to do a post-wedding evaluation from the grave. An extra salty tear accumulated in his eye as Dorian looked at the five golden stars and read along in his head:

WONDERFUL TOP-NOTCH EXPERIENCE! Jinx is truly everything I could've hoped for. While planning my wedding day massacre, I had many questions. There always seemed like there were a million things that could go wrong. But as I sit here on the eve of my wedding, I have full confidence in the arrangement. The intricate setup was plotted out methodically and cleverly masked with the utmost thought and attention to detail. We have some terrible things planned for tomorrow, but thanks to Jinx, my wildest fantasies will all be played out in great detail. They will all be brought to light and remembered forever. I'll always love you Jinx! Five fucking stars, I highly recommend!

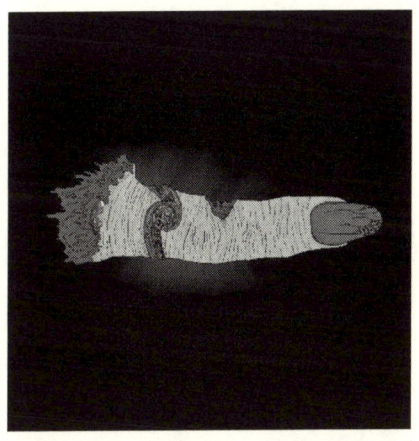

ABOUT THE AUTHOR

Aron Beauregard is a Splatterpunk Award nominated author who finds crime and mass murder incredibly intriguing. He has studied the subject in depth and has a fascination with what pushes people to the edge. There are many questions that float around in his mind: What can possibly drive a person to slaughter an enormous group of strangers? How can people be so ruthless? What is the tipping point for these acts of depravity? McDonalds or Burger King? Stay tuned to find out more about the sinister criminal underbelly of society and the never-ending fountain of horrors that bleed from his inkwell.

To learn about the extremely disturbing backstory around Dorian's internet viewing of "The Best New Kids," read the final story in the horror collection "Dark Assembly," titled "Last Days in Honduras." If you dare...

Made in the USA
Middletown, DE
15 February 2026

28722734R00151